YOU DON'T LOVE YOURSELF

BY THE SAME AUTHOR

FICTION

Tropisms

Portrait of a Man Unknown

Martereau

The Planetarium

The Golden Fruits

Between Life and Death

Do You Hear Them?

"Fools Say"

NONFICTION

The Age Of Suspicion: Essays on the Novel

The Use of Speech

Childhood

DRAMA

Collected Plays

YOU DON'T LOVE YOURSELF

A NOVEL

NATHALIE SARRAUTE

Translated by BARBARA WRIGHT
in consultation with the author

George Braziller, Inc.   New York

Published in the U.S. in 1990 by George Braziller, Inc.

Originally published in France in 1989 as *Tu ne t'aimes pas* by
Editions Gallimard, 5 rue Sébastien-Bottin, 75341 Paris.

© 1989 Editions Gallimard.
© 1990 English translation, by George Braziller, Inc.

For further information, address the publisher:
George Braziller, Inc.
60 Madison Avenue
New York, NY 10010

Library of Congress Cataloging-in-Publication Data

Sarraute, Nathalie.
[Tu ne t'aimes pas.   English]
You don't love yourself/by Nathalie Sarraute; translated by
Barbara Wright in consultation with the author.
p.   cm.
Translation of: Tu ne t'aimes pas.
ISBN 0-8076-1254-5: $17.95
I. Title.
PQ2637.A783T813   1990
843'.914—dc20   90-44526
                                                          CIP

Cover design by Jacqueline Schuman
Text design by Maureen O'Brien/MODINO

Printed in the United States of America

First edition

YOU DON'T LOVE YOURSELF

"You don't love yourself." But what does that mean? How is that possible? You don't love yourself? Who doesn't love whom?

You, of course... you, the only one they were talking to.

Me? Only me? Not all the rest of you who are me?... and there are so many of us... "a complex personality"... like every other... Who is supposed to love whom, then, in all this?

But they told you: "You don't love yourself." You... The one who showed yourself to them, the one who volunteered, you wanted to be the one on duty... you went up to them... as if you were not merely one of our possible personifications, one of our virtualities... you broke away from us, you put yourself forward as our sole representative... you said "I"...

We all do that all the time. What else can we do? Every time one of us shows himself to the outside world he designates himself as "I," as "me"... as if he were the only one, as if you didn't exist...

What are you so surprised at, then... Who is I? Who doesn't love whom? But *I*, who am *I*? But I am only one among us, a small fragment... Anyone might think that this was the first time you have been taken for us all...

I don't know why, but I felt your presence more strongly than usual... you were there, around...

Of course, we were a little restless, we were ill at ease, embarrassed... Not all of us, though... This "we" doesn't apply to us all... We never turn out in full force... there are always some of us who are dozing, lazing, relaxing, wandering... this "we" can only refer to the ones who were there when you came out with that remark, the ones who are made ill at ease by that sort of performance, they feel they're being attacked...

You ought to have stopped me...

How very easy, when one of us suddenly breaks away from the rest of us, thrusts himself forward... you had taken it upon yourself to be our spokesman, you wouldn't let anyone else get a word in edgeways... we couldn't interrupt the flow of words streaming from you to them, which they were absorbing, like a magic philter that made one of those images appear in front of them... look at it...

I'd rather not.

But you must... now that you've come back to yourself, or rather, to us again, now that we're here, among ourselves, in our innermost being, you must look again at what you showed them, that form you gave rise to in them, one of the ones they are used to, of classic simplicity... it may prevent you from exposing yourself to them in future... Try, make an effort...

I can't see very well...

But all the same, like us you can manage to call to mind that face, our face, which you showed them... not one of those we see in the mirror, in photographs, not one of those composed faces, staring eyes, features arranged to their best advantage... but that flattened face with, on its slackly-stretched lips, in its eyes, something humble, ashamed... let us listen to our voice... no, it's true, we can't hear it... but even so we can perceive the inflections you put into it... and the words it carries... which words?... pointless to try to retrieve exactly the same ones... it's that character you must look at again, the one you presented to them... a buffoon, a grotesque clown... always putting his foot in it... and yet timid, defenseless... you sighed... "Ah, what can you expect, that's the way I am, always the same mistakes... Incorrigible... Ever since I was a child I've always admired, I've always been envious of the people who have the luck... not to be like me..."

All right, let's not go on about it... It needed a mischievous touch... we were so bored... I was trying to amuse them, to amuse myself a little at my own expense... no, at whose expense? what am I talking about? That's where such expressions lead... Not at "my own" expense... I wasn't the only one... You were there too, you who are also part of "me," of what is so called, you who are deserving, courageous, you who are skillful... I thought that they, over there, outside, could see you... well, that they suspected your existence...

You were crediting them with a lot... they don't look so far... One of them wanted to stop you... they were perhaps a little embarrassed for you, in spite of their laughter... to set you right, to remind you of the conventions, of good manners, so he stepped forward... you remember how he came up from behind, he put his hand on your shoulder, on our shoulder... and he said in a pitying, rather sorrowful tone... "You know what's the trouble with you? You don't love yourself"... as if not loving oneself were a defect, a disease... Every one of them is healthy, normal, every one of them loves himself, but we... we don't love ourselves.

Most amazing... we had never noticed that before... we would never have suspected it, it took that outburst of yours to make it apparent to us for the first time: that "you don't love yourself," which was meant only for you, you who were appearing to them, you whom they saw, it should be applied to us, yes, that's right, to *us*, of whom you are a part, to us who allowed you to exhibit yourself, to us who were there with you: *we* don't love ourselves...

And yet there are moments when some of us go on a little voyage of discovery outside, and from there, taking up their position at a distance, they examine themselves... and they like what they see...

But they haven't time to start to love themselves... the moment they're back home with us they lose themselves amongst us again, they melt into the crowd...

And that crowd—how can it love itself? or hate itself, for that matter?... It's really difficult to understand.

But it must be delightful to love oneself... Is there any sort of love that is more reliable, more constant, comforting, than that... In comparison with that love, even the famous maternal love... and then, it has one advantage that no other love has: it will only die when we do, we are sure of not surviving it.

People who love themselves are very lucky... But it isn't luck... that's what they'll tell us... it's a natural state, they love themselves without even thinking about it, they love themselves effortlessly... otherwise, how can we live?

Yes indeed, how?

Well, just the way we do live. Not so badly, after all... we get by...

But people who love themselves live better.

That's certain... and they are in the majority. You were an exception... it attracted their attention.

That's because I was acting the clown. I wanted to be a buffoon... you know very well that I have a tendency that way... all of a sudden it comes over me... it seems they don't have anyone to play that part. Or perhaps, if one of them were willing to risk it, those who are dignified, prudent, would be strong enough to prevent him from coming forward... But from there to believing that they love themselves...

6

With some of them, though, when you come to think of it, it's obvious...

Do they truly love themselves? Is it what's really called loving? But how do they manage it?

It's very simple. They feel that all the elements they are composed of are indissolubly welded together, all of them without distinction... the charming ones and the ugly ones, the bad ones and the good ones, and that compact whole they call "I" or "me" possesses the faculty of duplicating itself, of looking at itself from outside, and what it sees—that "I"—it loves.
Exactly what happens to us when we are looking at other people, people who are not us—and whom we love... *They* love themselves too...

It really is the most enviable of gifts... which the good fairies gave them at birth... But us, no, they didn't give it to us.

Not surprising, disadvantaged as we are, untalented, that...

Oh yes, talk about untalented...

But don't you think that above all they were helped... that since their childhood people looked on them with love, with admiration... they saw themselves reflected in other people's eyes... and that image...

No... that's precisely one of our deficiencies... the images of ourselves that other people send back to us— we can't manage to see ourselves in them...

Yes, you the demolisher... you always want to deform these images, to destroy them... to stop them from sticking to us, from adhering all over...

But most of the time you don't even need to intervene, they slide over us, they don't adhere, everything that moves in us makes them shift, they can't settle.

That's the whole point. What can we do to make an image of ourselves stick all over us, take shape, remain fixed long enough...

Yes, for us to be able to contemplate it...

A beautiful image...

Oh, not even beautiful... an image of ourselves that we would love just as it is...

That wouldn't be transformed into an enormous shifting mass... which contains everything... in which so many dissimilar things collide, destroy each other...

Let's try to remember... have we never spoken to anybody about this particularity?

8

Not to say, this infirmity...

We did try. You who always go straight up to people and ask them questions just like that, point-blank...

When I hear you, I curl up, I shrink back into ourselves as far as I can go, I'm always expecting you to be snubbed...

You said... it was crazy... "Listen, I wanted to ask you... Do you, inside yourself, well, in your inmost depths, do you have the impression... but I really do mean:—in your innermost recesses, that you can manage to see yourself with some degree of clarity... do you have the impression that you know who you are..."

Remember how his "frank," "open," "kindly" gaze... a look which had actually encouraged that kind of question... how it became even more open... "What did you say? Have I misunderstood you? You're asking me whether I know who I am? Must I tell you?" "Oh yes..." "Well, I'm a man of fifty, the father of a family, of Irish origin... My profession..." "No, not that... not that sort of thing, I too know that about myself... What I wanted to know was... it's hard to explain... whether you feel that you are a very compact and unified whole, endowed with such and such qualities and, of course, defects... but forming a whole... a clearly-defined whole that you can look at from outside... well, that you project in front of yourself..." "Ah, that, yes. And when I observe myself carefully, I always see in myself... you see, it's quite complicated... there are two men in me, sometimes I'm the one and sometimes the other, not both at the same time... I get that from my grandfather, he always used to say: 'There's a monk and a banker in me'..." "That's right. Like Dr. Jekyll and Mr. Hyde, two contradictory beings..." "Yes, although I have to admit that as regards a Mr. Hyde in me... obviously nobody's perfect... but I don't believe..." "Oh, that wasn't what I meant, I just wanted to point out that there were two people in you... That's very few..."

You remember his astonishment... "That's few? Are there more in you?"

And you, shamefacedly... "Oh yes, there are as many... as there are stars in the sky... others are always appearing whose existence no one suspected... So you see, I've given up, I am the entire universe, all its virtualities, all its potentialities... the eye can't perceive it, it extends to infinity..."

It made us want to laugh, he seemed so alarmed... He moved away, withdrew into his shell, and let these words escape him: "Have you never spoken of this to anyone?" You shook your head... "No, only to you..." "I'm not really the right person, you know, that kind of loss of the feeling of myself... or that proliferation... I don't know... these are questions... you ought to discuss them with someone more competent..."

In short, a total fiasco. It was only to be expected... but you're incorrigible...

No, you know very well that since that day I have never again risked...

You've run other risks... we tremble every time it comes over you... but we can never manage to transfer our trembling into your voice... which makes your attitude even more embarrassing... but you carry us along with you, it's impossible to resist you...

And afterwards, when you've calmed down and we're home again, it's useless for us to remonstrate with you... You promise not to do it again... For a short time no one who goes out is guilty of the slightest imprudence... the only ones who show themselves outside are those who stand on their dignity... no more of those questions, ever...

At least that particular question has never been asked since. But now, after that "You don't love yourself," if we were to go and ask them: "Tell me, how do you go about loving yourselves?" you can imagine how they would look... Just to think about it...

No point in trying. We ought to make the effort to find out for ourselves...

With a lot of them, this love can't be seen outside... they look just like us, even though they're so different... in any case in this respect, seeing that we are the exception...

We ought to get the people in whom it does show to reveal themselves to us. There are plenty of models...

That one over there... as the saying goes, he looks the part. Pink and plump. Chubby-cheeked, and as if swollen...

No, not him. He's "too good to be true"... Too crude. A painted wax doll who radiates self-satisfaction. He isn't the one we need...

Who, then?

We'll have to wait... stay on the lookout... Not let ourselves be sidetracked... every one of us must be prepared...

Something is coming into view...

Yes, what is it?

For the moment it's only a hand. The man it belongs to, we can't see him, he's in the shade... It's only his hand there in the bright light in front of us... a long, rather gnarled hand with very short nails...

And now in his barely-visible face too, not even his eyes... just his gaze...

He's gazing intently at his hand on the table.

And so much love in his gaze... That's the way it is with people who love themselves... their love goes first to everything they can see that belongs to them... their hands, their feet, their forearms... and then their reflection in the mirror...

And we? Haven't there been moments when we too...

Brief moments, more of astonishment... Is that really me?... But very soon another and yet another reflection appeared... And then we were busy looking elsewhere so we didn't stop to contemplate...

In his gaze, as in that of lovers, everything there is in him of admiration, of tenderness, is poured out on to his hand... he spreads his fingers the better to contemplate every one of them, he moves them to watch them coming to life... A real miracle, that hand... one of the wonders of creation...

Yes, but our hand, ours too, when we think about it...

But that's just it, we don't think about it. We would never take it into our head to spread it out on the table like his. Why should we do that? Our hands are utilitarian objects, utensils limited to their function, they have no purpose here...

14

And the whole of our body—at this moment we don't feel its presence, it's as if it didn't exist... and there's nothing else in us but that; whereas his hand—every detail of his long, greyish fingers, with a few black hairs on the third phalanx, his smooth, pink nails cut straight across... and his gaze, dripping with tenderness, resting on it... And then we hear the words he utters...

And these words immediately arouse in us... like the drum roll that makes soldiers come running... They stand rigidly, with staring eyes, in the parade ground... A grand courtyard, an esplanade where we watch him swaggering...

We are now no more than a gaze fixed on him, ears heedful of his orders...

Not orders shouted out loud... this is where the comparison stops... his words insinuate themselves into us softly, and force us to...

Yes, rather than orders, implicit threats of sanctions... they exercise a strange fascination over us and force us to gaze at him without blinking, without looking away for a second...

And in any case, looking away at what? Nothing exists except what he obliges us to see...

We can imagine our smile full of respectful sympathy, our eyes opening even wider in amazement, our appreciative nod as he speaks... "Yes, every day when I get up I have to start by drinking a plateful of soup... Thick, like my grandfather did every day of his life... And about an hour later, a cup of very strong coffee... And then, one after the other two cigarettes... the effect is only produced after the second one..." He places his hand over his stomach, he smiles... the accomplice of his intestines "which perform in-va-ri-a-bly..." he draws out the word, he stresses every syllable in tones of satisfaction, of gratitude... "In-va-ri-a-bly... Never fail..." Here he stops... And our perfect docility prevents us from leaving him. Out of the question, in his presence, for us to wander...

To return to ourselves... And yet with us too, two cigarettes... and even just one, sometimes... It's probably a more frequent effect than people think...

But nothing of that sort insinuated itself into us at that moment. No comparison between him and anyone else...

Doesn't it seem, though, that even at that moment a fleeting memory...

Soon rejected... not worth considering, something colorless, insignificant... a poor, barely-visible creature

16

relegated to the sidelines, whereas in the center of the room a dazzling beauty, the queen of the ball... everyone's gaze concentrated on her...

Which reminds us that we were not the only ones looking at him, listening to him. A few people were sitting like us at that table... they too were contemplating him in silence...

But then... those people who were so watchful and so silent—weren't they like us? Weren't they, too, like us?...

Ceasing to exist in his presence?

Would they not love themselves? Then we wouldn't be an exception?

You, who find exploring so amusing, you, our researcher, our detective, make an effort, we're wandering... Don't they love themselves? Not they, either?

Oh yes, they love themselves all right... That's what attracts them to him, that's what brings them together round him: the great love he has for himself... the love he bears for himself helps them to love themselves even better...

But how? What are you talking about?

Wait, don't rush me... you'll muddle everything up... Let's first try to have another look at the scene...

We are there, contemplating, listening to the person making an exhibition of himself...

The one who loves himself...

Yes... this is the moment when, as they say, he's "the cynosure of all eyes"... We are only an empty space in which he can parade...

But aren't all the others around him just like that?

No, let's take a good look at them again... Can't we see in them, rising up in them, something that reaches out... that grasps, hoards inside themselves, piles up in their treasure house, in their safes, the presents the person who loves himself is busy distributing so generously?

That's true... the love people have for themselves produces effects like that... Anyone who loves himself so intensely transforms everything that emanates from him into wealth... everything without exception... his slightest manifestations, sketches, rough drafts, gossip, ramblings, babblings, greetings cards, name written in his own hand, account books, the effect of cigarettes on the functioning of his intestines...

18

But doesn't he first have to have distinguished himself by some great deed? To have produced a masterpiece?

No, that's just it. It's his self-love that must come first, providing of course that it is a great love... a love that has always been perfect... such a love will transform what he then does into a masterpiece...

That love oozes out of the man who came and served us as a model, it flows out of the way he looks at himself... that love covers, envelops... a wrapping worthy of the objects he offers to anyone capable of appreciating them... Who will preserve them piously...

That's right... like decorations, like diplomas which they frame... It will fortify, magnify their self-love...

How proudly they will later exhibit these gifts they have received from the person who loves himself, these honors...

But on one condition: those who benefit from these gifts must already love themselves, otherwise...

Of course, otherwise, if there is nothing in them that reaches out, nothing that grasps, takes away, hoards, preserves... if there is no treasure house in

19

them, no safe, nowhere to hang decorations, diplomas...

If they are like us, a space open on all sides, which
all these beautiful presents merely traverse...

What a waste... That's what comes of not loving
yourself...

I must confess... you may have forgotten... it did
once happen to me to grasp one of these gifts in passing... and then...

What? Did you exhibit the two cigarettes in front
of the others? the soup? the coffee? or what else?

You know very well I didn't. I wouldn't be one of
us.

That's true, which of us could?...

Wait, he's right... I remember... he broke away
from us, he stepped forward... we were amazed...

Yes, that day, when all of a sudden you told us
what had been said to you by...

Not that one... another... and *what* another!... to
say that he loves himself is putting it too mildly... he

20

worships himself... and all around him his worshippers... but I wasn't one of them...

We respect his work, that's all, but as for the man himself...

We didn't think much of him...

So I reported on what he told me... only on his method of working, not on the man himself... I wasn't trying to magnify us... no, not at all...

You had mentioned his name.

I had to, to back up my arguments about what he himself had confided in me...

Ah, in that case...

Yes, what we were expecting did happen...

They forgot about his work, they were only interested then in looking at what you were displaying to them, what you had received from him, that honor...

That wasn't at all what I wanted to show them, I hadn't even thought about it.

But that was what they saw. It's coming back to us now...

Yes, the way they looked when you mentioned his name... their appreciation... a little surprised... you've grown up, you've become someone who has had the honor of meeting... who has heard his words from his own mouth... who has taken them away and preserved them...

And all of us imbricated with you... all of us trapped... it took us years to forgive you for that, to stop reproaching ourselves for not having held you back...

We finally forgot...

It wasn't until it came back to me...

But what's the use of hiding the truth... We have been moved over to their side for ever... for them, we are the person who received that high honor, that diploma...

Somewhere, over there, inside them, when we appear, that's what we are, someone who has received a diploma, a decoration...

We...

Yes, we... reduced to that...

We who are so numerous... illimitable... immeasurable...

22

How can the others, when they look inside themselves, manage to find their way around? They are like us, though, every one of them... such infinities... anyone can see that from what sometimes comes out of them that is so surprising, unpredictable... a complete contrast all of a sudden with what we previously saw...

Yes, but do they feel it?

Judging by the one you went and questioned... he was so proud of having discovered two opposing people in himself... so amazed that you thought that so few...

How do they manage to feel so clear-cut, so simple?

They must train themselves for it very early... they are very powerfully helped towards it from their earliest childhood... The most gifted among them, the most precocious ones, already see themselves as everyone else sees them: as babies... then as little boys, as little girls, as tomboys...

Once they've got into the habit of feeling themselves to be the way they are seen, they keep it for ever... at every stage in their lives they feel they are women, men...

And nothing more. "Real" women, "real" men... who conform as closely as possible to the models...

Yes, "real" even down to their slightest gestures, their voices, their intonation...

And to their passions, their attachments...

If they stopped being "real," what would they be like? We might be most surprised...

There are certainly some who feel they are a mixture of man and woman... but always the simplest of mixtures...

24

As for old people... well, they have often been so well trained throughout their long lives to feel "real," that in the end they can't manage to be anything other than that: really perfect models... some of them must think they deserve to be seen as "the very image of old age."

And anyway, they often get great satisfaction from it, pride...

But we... Are we, then, for the people who see us, so disconcerting, unclear, muddled?

Certainly not. You know very well how zealously, how eagerly we sometimes muster up within ourselves those of us who make us most resemble what we ought to feel we are...

We quite naturally feel we are "real" women, "real" men, "real" fathers, mothers, sons, daughters, grandparents...

Those in us who compose them take power, they ostracize all the others, push them into dark corners where they remain inactive, dozing, forgotten...

But not for long... they are always somewhere there in us... they may wake up at any moment and come and intrude, upset everything... Then we wouldn't be quite sure who we are... It would make them laugh, the people who observe us from outside, if they could see what we see in ourselves at times... so many lively young people and adolescents gathered together in "old fogeys," and so many old men in young people... and everywhere so many children...

Yes, some very strange distributions of populations...

Look whom I've brought... he's come back to me... there are more of them than we think... but we've already had some dealings with this one... When he was still only a small child he managed the *tour de force* of producing a self-portrait.

Or rather a statue of himself, which he always carried within himself...

Like people who still have a bullet, a piece of shrapnel in their bodies...

Or something just as hard, as solid... but this isn't like a bit of metal that might have remained stuck somewhere inside him. This statue of himself occupies the whole of him, there's no room in him for anything else.

Shall we ever understand how he went about it?

It's difficult... He said he had copied it from something he found in children's books... They described children who would later become great geniuses. He wanted to be one too. So he created a statue of the future genius that he would be. And he became it.

They were one and the same, his statue and himself. So they grew up together...

And later they became a great genius, his statue and he.

But hadn't he all the time had to eliminate everything that appeared in him that was not worthy of being a part of his construction, that might have damaged his statue?

What a lot of elements he must have had to discard, to throw on the scrap heap...

Oh no, less than one might think. Everything that is idle, dreamy, "good for nothing," vain, ungrateful, vindictive, cowardly, mean... in fact everything that can more or less be found in us all and which is everywhere despised and obliged to conceal itself... all this in him could be used to erect, to perfect his statue, to throw its facets into relief, to bring sparkle into its diverse, improbable, and even shocking aspects, always so delightful to contemplate when they are those of a great genius...

What nostalgia that arouses in us, doesn't it? What a pleasure it would be to imitate him...

But are you mad? But you're not serious? Imitate him? Us?

No... not by constructing such a superb statue... But just a statue... however modest...

Oh yes, what a relief...

And what opportunities... we could describe that statue, talk about it...

We could "tell about ourselves"... as they say about someone "Oh, tell me about him, I would so like to know him..."

We would "tell about ourselves" in that way...

In some cases, when other people are so nicely, so confidently, so frankly telling about themselves... one feels guilty at receiving so much without giving anything in return...

They must think that no exchange is possible with us, that we are arrogant, secretive...

Sometimes it's very embarrassing...

It embarrasses me so much that I can't stand it... I start "telling about myself"...

Well yes. And we let you do it, show yourself, speak in our name... come out with a lot of nonsense...

No, not nonsense... more like untruths...

Not at all, when I told about how I don't get attached to objects... how without batting an eyelid I had seen my entire house disappear... with all its contents... it was true. Absolutely. But you were there all around, fidgeting, murmuring... "And what about when the teapot was lost... and the old coffee grinder... and when the ceiling lamp got broken..."

Weren't we all, even you, upset? didn't we look everywhere? our heart was beating... anyone might have thought a catastrophe had happened to us... is that true or is that untrue?

30

Come on, it's no use insisting...

There's no way of opening one's mouth...

And then when some of us try to stick adjectives on ourself...

Yes, qualifiers...

It takes courage...

Not courage: nerve. To have the nerve to saddle us with words like happy-go-lucky, optimistic... you remember...

You had the nerve to say: "Personally, you know, I'm more the happy-go-lucky type..." What an outburst there was then...

All the dozing anxiety-carriers, the ones we take tranquilizers for, suddenly sat up... you could hear them whispering on all sides... happy-go-lucky?... did you say happy-go-lucky? When at times whole tidal waves of anxiety break over us, we go rolling over, choking...

That's when we hang on to our old teapots... cling on to our ceiling lamps...

But what's the use of going on?

All the same, let's remember that time when it did happen, as the outside pressure was so great, when we tried to get together and show a splendid "I" that was presentable, really solid...

We managed to say in a confident voice: "You know, that's the way I am..."

"Full of contradictions, of course..." This, all the same, we were forced to add by those of us who have scruples...

"Yes, that's the way I am... full of contradictions, of course, but actually on the whole, I am..."

What? Who can remember clearly what that "I" was?

It was a good "I," a good fellow... "I never have any wish to take my revenge..."

And at that moment, none of us turned a hair...

But have any of us ever felt the desire for vengeance?

32

We'd have to search...

It looks as if we distanced ourselves, that's all...

Yes, out of disgust...

And also out of fear...

But isn't that one way of taking one's revenge?

We had banished for ever the one who committed the offense...

But only banished him from us. Everywhere else the offender is still living very comfortably, is still in the best of health...

But anyway, that day, "I never have any wish to take my revenge" went off without mishap...

That day we all showed a great deal of goodwill.

It was amusing, it was very exhilarating, that construction... We were quite excited...

We added this... and then that...

Like the pipe someone sticks in the middle of the face... the felt hat he puts on the head...

Yes, of a snowman...

How quickly, when he was back amongst us on his own, he melted...

That's our statue.

It's the absence of frontiers, of boundaries around us... our place is open to all comers...

Not like his place, the person who loves himself... *He* surrounds himself with defensive walls...

Himself, and everything that even remotely belongs to him... his familiar circle, his ancestors and descendants, his pets...

It would make a long list, everything he keeps out of harm's way behind deep moats, parapet walks, watchtowers where sentries are always on the lookout...

When someone from outside arrives... he saw him coming a long way off... he examines him with the greatest circumspection. What is he bringing with him? What is it? But it's a truth... of the kind you "come out with" when you say: "I told him a few home truths"... and he comes out with it and wants to apply it to the master of the house or to one of his children or grandchildren...

Who does he take himself for, though? Has he got a warrant? A special permit? Is he a pedagogue or a psychiatrist called here to give his opinion?

No, not at all, he's an amateur who thinks he can do anything he likes. So he's forcibly seized and thrown out, or shown the door with polite scorn...

But what are we dreaming up? Who, unasked, would come out with that sort of home truth to anyone who loves himself?

Whereas with us there is no checkpoint... these truths enter quite freely...

It could be one about some trait in our character... or about our behavior...

It's of no importance... this truth always attracts some of us... they examine it inquisitively, tranquilly, but they soon lose sight of it... once it has entered into us it gets lost among other truths... they are so numerous and so diverse...

But when this truth has to be applied to one of our familiar circle, someone with whom we are linked by very strong bonds of affection, then something surprising occurs... We come rushing up from all sides... Quick, we want to see that truth, show it to us!

We don't stop to take a close look at the person who has brought it... For us, he is merely the bearer of the truth... of an irrefutable truth...

He may be a representative of the *vox populi*...

Which gives his truth such power!

Or he may be someone who has a reputation for subtlety... or someone who merely possesses elementary common sense... or someone who lacks it... and in that case he certainly has the visionary gifts of the insane... in short, just about anyone gets transformed into a profound psychologist, a clairvoyant, an oracle...

Out of our seething mass an "I" steps forward, we propel him outside... Like us, trembling, panting, he asks: "Really? You think Robert... yes... is... what?... secretive! I'd never noticed that, we can be so wrong about people we're fond of... But what makes you think that? But why, exactly?"

We become even more excited when the reply isn't immediately forthcoming...

Or doesn't come at all... is replaced by an evasive "Oh, I don't know," full of disturbing possibilities...

And then we have to look, we have to find out for ourselves... We make him appear before us... No need to say Robert! Here, among ourselves, we don't pronounce his name... just one of his gestures, a movement of his neck, of his hand brushing back the lock of hair that always falls over his forehead, the shape of his ear, his thumbnail... and here he is, he's back with us...

And behind him, or rather inside him, spreading... immense...

But not infinite, as in us...

It's more like an ocean... shores, always the same ones, surround him, contain him...

But while we fix him with our gaze, he hardens, takes shape... Every feature, every detail of his face stands out so clearly...

Like those on the face of a stranger when we're getting our first impression of him...

38

Which they say is the correct one...

When we look at him, this stranger, with all our faculties of observation aroused, all our instinct of self-preservation on the alert...

And in that new face, at the corner of its lips, where they meet...

It's obvious, something is curled up there... It's what might be called... it's what *is* called... it's secretiveness...

And the ocean has grown deeper, narrower, in him...

The Atlantic has become the Dead Sea.

Or rather, the sea of Hypocrisy...

It becomes visible in his eyes...

It's a sly gaze...

Some of us, the ones who even in such cases keep their wits about them...

There aren't very many of them...

They dare to murmur: "But we have never seen him act in a way that could be called hypocritical... does anyone remember anything of the sort?..."

Our researchers immediately hunt everywhere, report... and we get together to look into the matter... It's true, we'd forgotten it, his way of avoiding discussions, of acquiescing... he avoids contradicting... He stands on his dignity... Which doesn't mean that he isn't thinking... He disguises...

Which of us hadn't already noticed it? But we'd buried it deep...

We're so blind... so naïve...

We're so craven... We're so afraid of feeling it embed itself in us... the truth...

Oh, that's enough, it hurts...

Even when the pain has gradually subsided, even when other truths have come and replaced it, that particular truth returns when you least expect it and curls up in that movement of his lips... in his acquiescence... in his prudent, scornful retreat... or in anything else... that we weren't expecting...

But wasn't it amusing to see ourselves recounting our misadventure to one of the people who love themselves...

Perhaps to ask him to comfort us...

Or to help us conquer that truth...

No, not that, we know it's invincible.

The amusing thing was his amazement. He couldn't get over it. He couldn't believe his ears...

And that was from our very first words... he didn't let us get as far as "Robert is secretive"... He stopped us the moment we said... well, the moment the "I" who was speaking in our name told him that someone had thought... "What? Who? Who thought what? Who dared? How could you have allowed?..." Our "I" blushes, stammers... "But he saw the truth..." "The truth? And he had the audacity to point it out to you?" "But I wanted to see it..." "You wanted..." the one who loves himself collapses on to his chair, looking dazed... "You wanted... you let someone close to you be attacked..." "But that's of no importance. The truth must... what can we do against it?... You wouldn't have allowed?..." "*I?* allowed *anyone* to approach... to dare... when one of my people is concerned... No, at the very idea..." he wipes his forehead... "that an insolent, crazy fellow should allow himself in my presence..." In his gaze, which becomes more and more probing, in his smile, there appears something like a touch of contempt, of mockery... "Well, you know, I feel sorry for you!"

"Twenty years of happiness... Well yes... I've had that..." a precious stone they bring out of their jewel case and get us to admire... "Twenty years of happiness..."

A jewel with which they adorn themselves in front of us...

Thus embellished, they contemplate themselves... they consider themselves even more worthy of their self-love...

Because "Twenty years of happiness" reveals all kinds of qualities...

A pure, harmonious, generous soul...

And also a certain combination of circumstances, as they readily acknowledge: "I've been lucky..." and the fact that they have been lucky only adds to their pride.

Heaven doesn't hand out its favors to just anyone...

Not to us, in any case. Even ten years, even one year of happiness... which of us, when he's on duty outside and tempted to show himself off, would ever dare to appear with that?

Just the very word "Happiness," when we try to see it more clearly, evokes such images in us...

Those of holiday brochures... A perfectly calm, perfectly blue sea, an unclouded sky...

And anyway, "Happiness" is often added to "unclouded," to emphasize even further its perfection, its perfect purity.

With us too, there *have* been moments...

When we seemed to be carried away, elevated, fused, merged, dissolved... We were beside ourselves...

44

We ought to have been able to come back to ourselves, find ourselves again, recover our self-possession, turn round, look at ourselves... what's going on in us?... what is it called, the thing that's happening to us?... to look for a suitable word among the ones we know... to choose Happiness and calmly declare that it is moments of Happiness we are now living through...

But that's precisely what we find impossible...

So no name brought in from outside has been applied to these moments... They haven't been baptized... they remain forever in limbo...

When we try to retrieve them, now that they've gone, now that we're far away from them, they sometimes appear to us to be like incandescent points scattered here and there over vast, foggy expanses...

What a *tour de force* it is, then, to be able to give an immediate name to every one of these moments, to bring these scattered Happinesses together, to compress them, to make an enormous solid block of them... "Twenty years of Happiness..."

But we're digressing... "Twenty years of Happiness" isn't made up of bits and pieces joined end to end God knows how... Happiness isn't a name that has had to be sought in order to try and apply it to God knows

45

what... Happiness was there ready-made, known from the beginning, very visible from a long way off, spreading everywhere, offering itself, displaying its name, the most famous name of all, the most prestigious...

People who had been able to acquire Happiness and preserve it for twenty years had never stopped contemplating it since their childhood, they had been shown it from all angles, they had been taught to worship it, they knew that nothing more desirable exists on this earth...

It's natural that someone who loves himself, who's always busy taking good care of himself, should always strive for Happiness with all his strength...

But what kind of Happiness? Aren't there all kinds? for all tastes?

Yes. But the most famous, the most highly-prized, the ones that are offered by the most beautiful brochures, the ones with the best brand names, are not very numerous. They contain certain materials that are the height of luxury... Love, of course, a model, a perfect Love, and then Success, and then... But why waste our time enumerating what we have at our finger tips...

Inevitably, someone who loves himself feels unjustly deprived so long as he hasn't had it, this Happiness which other people possess, even though they are less deserving of it...

And then, when it *does* fall to his lot, how reassured he is... He knew very well that he was made for Happiness and that Happiness was made for him. Happiness is the environment that suits him. Happiness is his natural element.

Happiness is the air he breathes, and Happiness emanates from him...

But after "Twenty years of Happiness," what on earth can have happened? Is it possible to imagine that he emerged from it of his own accord? that he deserted it on purpose?

Of course not. Nothing but an equally great, equally extreme Unhappiness, as famous and respected as Happiness, can have snatched it away from someone who loves himself...

A noble Unhappiness equally worthy of him... which doesn't make him lose face... An Unhappiness that he can show...

Which is sometimes even becoming.

As becoming as Happiness.

But we mustn't be unkind. Why disparage people who love themselves?

The thing is, we sometimes feel so envious of them...

If you please, let's not allow ourselves to be side-tracked by these frivolities... Let's rather try to be with the others... like them... Let's imagine that we too are in it...

In Happiness? But how?

But just looking from the outside, without entering into it...

Then you don't want to remember that it *has* happened to us...

To be in Happiness? That of the brochures, of the blue sea? of the cloudless sky? Us!

Remember, though... there are some of us... so far they've been keeping quiet, they've been hiding... but look at them now, they're coming back... You admit that you have striven for Happiness... and how nostalgically... you went towards it...

We were drawn into it... you know how influenceable, how credulous we are... And then all those advertisements, that continual propaganda, those famous models paraded, the advice, the encouragement, the tales told by people who are there... we couldn't resist it... And anyway, you others who are so strong, who don't believe everything you're told, you followed us...

You should rather say that you dragged us along with you, aided by the people outside, our relations, our parents, our friends... they enveloped us in what flowed out of their looks, their words...

So much hope, approval, emotion, admiration... we were completely stuck, softened, we let ourselves be pushed... but the moment we were admitted there we felt ill at ease...

In that imposing, sumptuous place with the name it bears... Happiness. Such a famous name... we were intimidated, tense... we weren't used to...

Humble people removed from their humble life and invited to a royal palace, to an elegant party... we didn't have the beautiful manners... that perfect naturalness, that freedom...

When we knew that that was what it was, the Happiness we had heard so much about, and that we were in Happiness, in which everything must remain so beautiful, of impeccable beauty... we were afraid we might damage something, disturb something... that made us even clumsier than we usually are, when we are not in it, in Happiness...

When we don't know where we are...

Being shut in there made us suffer from something like claustrophobia at times... we wanted to get out...

Yes, to get out of Happiness! But the people outside were keeping all the exits closed... they frightened us... To get out of Happiness, is that what you want? But are you forgetting what happens to the people who get out of it? What's lying in wait for them?

After that we made no more attempts to escape... we too managed to appear to be a model that people contemplate, in whom the people outside find inspiration...

The wolf disguised as the grandmother...

Ah, that was bound to happen... obviously, you're here too... you who spend your whole time digging up our shortcomings and pointing them out to us, our "undesirable elements"... all those little rascals, those wrongdoers...

You could even say: those murderers...

Fortunately they are only in embryo.

In any case, to see them established in Happiness when they aren't worth the rope to hang them by...

You were there quaking... we really don't deserve it... this adventure will turn out badly, we shall be thrown out, out of Happiness... it's really frightening...

One has to ward off the evil eye...

We heard you touching wood all the time... exasperating little tapping sounds...

Anyway, it wasn't long before such confusion reigned among us... such agitation... a real outburst...

Mingled with the apprehensive tapping sounds was the contemptuous laughter of those of us who are irritated by Happiness and its perfection, they don't believe in it... they were impatiently trying to touch, to search, to poke their noses into everything... they wanted to see it with their own eyes, to inspect it thoroughly... they got hold of this or that, they picked it up, examined it... *This*—in Happiness? You must be joking! they went to a corner and grabbed... And this? What's this? What's hiding here?... but it's tedium... and what tedium, just look at this, and they tried to drag a great big grey rubber doll out of its hiding-place... What are we supposed to do with this? but it's no use our trying to pull it out, it must be stuck somewhere, it's so heavy, sluggish...

And those of us who are possessed by the spirit of contradiction... they bridle, they shout out: Happiness isn't here... the name has been usurped... there's nothing here of what that name is supposed to designate. Ah, *we* have never been intimidated by an excess of magnificence, obsessed by that great name... We know, we have always known, it's... you know what it is, your Happiness? its real name is Castle in Spain.

And our "eternal children," who naturally want to amuse themselves by destroying their toy: they savagely demolish Happiness bit by bit, to see what it's made of... and we soon find ourselves surrounded by shapeless scraps, stuffing, there's sawdust and bran all over the place...

And the ones who creep along cautiously, they're afraid they're going to be stopped... it's towards the suffering lying in wait outside for people emerging from Happiness, it's towards suffering that they are irresistibly heading... it's their natural element... suffering is the air they breathe... they drag us with them... and there are more of us here than we knew... Who can hold us back?

And you who, at the least opportune moments, are always prompted by your kind hearts, you never stopped casting embarrassed glances out of the Happiness in which we were walking over the golden sands, in the middle of the palm trees, the date trees, in the exciting play of light and shade, of the pure, dazzling colors, among the noble, craggy faces of the old men, the mischievous, ingenuous little faces of the children... how exasperating you were when you forced us to notice those swollen bellies, those suppurating amputated limbs, those eyes hidden behind white specks... it was no use our calling you to order, appealing to your sense of decency, reproaching you for your vulgar sentimentality, your insensitivity to beauty, your egotism... it didn't bother you in the least that you never stopped making us jump, shudder, cringe, that you were tearing us apart, wrecking our unique excursion into what, without you, would have taken on the permanent shape, the light, the colors of Happiness...

And we must admit that none of us here can ever manage to forget its presence completely... however hard we try to ignore it... we always find it prowling around in the vicinity of Happiness...

There, especially... It seems as if its proximity to Happiness makes Happiness one of its favorite places... From time to time it approaches... just when we're thinking of it the least, it surreptitiously insinuates itself into the most innocuous thing, into something the least likely to arouse suspicion... one of those nondescript, inoffensive, even auspicious objects that Happiness contains... It amuses itself by making this object disappear, or else by blemishing it, by cracking it... and it inserts itself into the void it has left, through the blemish, the crack... It... disorder itself, the irreparable rupture, annihilation...

But what's the use of trying to capture it with words? You know very well that the words that could grasp it don't exist...

Perhaps if we simply call it by its name... Death...

It's odd... under that name we feel its presence less...

Yes, it's when it's something that can't be named, that can't be said, something that emanates from that blemish, those cracks, that it manages to unsettle... Happiness begins to falter...

And although nothing, absolutely nothing appears to be threatening it, it seems as if, under the most solidly-constructed Happiness, suddenly the earth is quaking...

Finally, what clearly emerges on our return from this brief excursion is that we—we are definitely not made for Happiness...

Not made... that's it... not made... it's always that defect in our construction... that malformation...

That flaw... we hadn't realized how serious it was, we hadn't had a chance to foresee its consequences when all of a sudden it was revealed to us by those surprising words... "You don't love yourself..."

If we had been able to feel it, that love for ourselves... then... why not?... with a bit of luck we too might have been able to live in Happiness...

Even for twenty years...

And even longer, why limit ourselves to that number?

It's our modesty again...

No, let's not deviate this time... let's try to join those who are "made for Happiness"... to feel what *they* feel, when they're in it...

How easy!

And yet some of us here find it quite easy to put themselves in the place of other people...

Yes, but what demands such a great effort is that this time we first need to fill ourselves with that love they have for themselves.

Just a moment... wait... I think I'm going to manage it... There... I've done it... I feel I love myself...

You don't say!

Silence! This is no time for joking. Let them go to work, those of us who are the most gifted...

In the first place, don't say "those" of us any more. Say: let him go to work... say "the one"... Yes. Me. I am only one. And not simply as one of our delegates whom we send when we have to present ourselves to the outside world... I am "one" inside myself. I am all of a piece. Yes. In my own eyes. Because I can see myself. I only have to stand aside a little... I look at myself: here I am. The sum of my qualities and defects...

Could you name them?

Of course. But what's the point? Don't distract me. I like this ensemble of qualities and defects. I don't want any others. I love myself the way I am. Yes, I love myself. I feel I deserve to be loved. I love myself...
And Happiness is here in front of me...

This time, shouldn't we look at what kind of Happiness?

It's enough for it to be what bears that name: Happiness... what everyone refers to as such... that it should

56

possess the qualities that make everyone who sees it recognize it at once, that everyone should exclaim "Ah, but that's Happiness!" And this Happiness is opening out in front of me... And as much as anyone, more than anyone, I deserve to enter into it. To remain there...

You can also say that without it, without Happiness, your life wouldn't be worth living.

Ah, thanks for coming to my aid...

Here it is then, the thing I was made for... the thing that gives all its value to my life... to any life... Happiness is in front of me... It's mine...It's opening up... I enter into it... Can you hear how everyone around is applauding me?

And now I'm in it, in Happiness. All my moments are passed in Happiness. Everything I do is done in Happiness... Do you follow me?

We're doing our best...

Look, I'm doing something or other...

As we are at every moment...

Yes, but for me, at the same time, there is that background... Happiness... everything becomes clear to me against that background... I never lose sight of it...

You see it the way one sees out of the corner of one's eye, without having to look round...

That's right... For instance, I'm watching a tennis match... I'm observing the court, the white lines, every movement the two players make, the trajectory, the spot where every ball lands... and at the same time I'm aware of what is there by my side... Happiness... Or else I get into a bus, I slide my ticket into the slot... and Happiness is with me, I can feel its presence...

Like a hummed accompaniment...

If you like... I can sense it wherever I am... whatever I'm doing. Happiness surrounds me on all sides. Everything takes on its flavor... the flavor of Happiness...

Like a wine we drink, knowing that it has been poured from a bottle of a choice vintage...

Please, no irony... Let me steep myself in this Happiness... soak myself in it... It's Happiness... That's what Happiness is... Everyone around me sees it, calls it that: Happiness. I am in Happiness... Happiness...

It has to be repeated like an incantation...

Like an exorcism...

58

An exorcism? But to ward off what? So you aren't managing to follow me...

That's true, what were we thinking of? In the state of Happiness you're in there can't be anything to fear... no evil eye...

No need to make little tapping sounds... to touch wood...

And of course never any need to crawl to get out of it...

Out of Happiness? Me? Get out of Happiness? Into suffering?

The thing is we sometimes forget, we can't always manage to remember that you love yourself... and suffering... obviously, that's what you want to avoid... And so, during the outing in the middle of the palm trees, the date trees, when all around the barouche the swollen bellies, the white specks...

But it was an outing into the very heart of Happiness... everything around was wearing its colors... that was where Happiness had one of its strongholds... my self-love flourished there...

That love and Happiness melted into one another... their union made them invincible... everything that might attack them retreated, withdrew...

And what if sometimes, when you aren't in one of those high places, what if as the days go by, here or there, in Happiness, a few minor imperfections...

Oh come on, I don't notice them... if there are any, a protective varnish flows out of my gaze and covers them up.

And of course there's never an inquisitive child who wants to see how it's made, who amuses himself by scratching off the varnish, who attacks it on all sides, dismantles, demolishes...

What child? You're forgetting that I'm an adult.

And what if the thing we daren't look at... which is always there, prowling around us... what if it insinuates itself everywhere, convulses the empty space hollowed out by a broken, mislaid object...

No, for me, a lost object leaves nothing behind it but an image... the sometimes obsessive, regretted image... of the object.

But you've distracted me again. I was trying to rediscover the sensation we have when we're living in Happiness... I'd already got there... but your continual interruptions...

We were only trying to help you...

Now I shall have to start all over again... Where'd I got to?

In the first place, you love yourself...

Yes, I've got that far... I love myself.

And Happiness is opening out in front of you.

Happiness... that's right... I'm established in it. My whole life bears its signs. Everyone who sees my life exclaims: "He has everything that makes up Happiness. There's nothing missing..." I am immersed in Happiness... My days are spent in Happiness... yes... wherever I am, Happiness is by my side... At every moment... whatever I'm doing... whatever I'm doing... And what exactly am I doing? I don't know...

We might perhaps suggest to you... Just take what you're doing at the moment... When you're trying to rediscover that sensation of Happiness... Happiness envelops you, protects you, it never leaves you... the people watching you see it, they say "Ah, that's Happiness, isn't it, when you can concentrate on rediscovering a sensation... When that is your only concern... when you haven't any others... That's the height of luxury..." And so you've got that far?

I think I shall get there, I shall rediscover that sensation of Happiness, now, this moment, while I'm searching... I'm putting everything I've got into it... I'd give anything to experience it... I'm going to get it... I've got it... no, I haven't got it... this isn't it... not Happiness...

What is it?

Oh, I don't know what to call it... Is it a worry? is it a terrible tension? is it a hope? is it a disappointment? is it...

Is it everything one might wish for, except Happiness? And to think that out of all of us it was you who were the most gifted... you who suggested yourself... you we were counting on!

But we mustn't despair. We ought rather to recognize that our inability "to experience Happiness" sometimes gives us a few advantages...

It's already an advantage not to be obliged to stick the name "Happiness" on every sensation that is still intact, alive... to crush it...

And not to see that smooth, shiny, tawdry varnish spread over everything... without a blemish, without a crack...

62

And that exhausting vigilance, that continual surveillance. A police regime. The slightest deviation, the slightest suspicion of freedom that might endanger Happiness, and one is called to order... brought back into Happiness bound hand and foot...

We must also remember the enjoyment we get from certain performances... What plays, what films could offer us scenes like those?

When they parade their Happiness in front of us...

And nothing budges in us... Not a trace, even in the most influenceable, the most credulous among us, the ones who are at the mercy of the most disappointing temptations... even with them, not a shade of nostalgia... not a trace of envy...

And yet, during one of those performances...

Yes, the lovers ostentatiously reaching out, joining their hands in front of us... gazing more and more deeply into each other's eyes as we look on... And we find it amusing to observe them... it's for our benefit that they're putting on that show... a beautiful shop window in which they display their happiness... It's amusing to observe so much naïveté, such certainty that they are giving us... how accurate these vulgar expressions can be... that they are giving us an eyeful...

A most curious, interesting production...

On one condition: that we remain at a distance, observe it without losing our self-possession.

When we're alone, nothing's easier...

Oh, easy... let's not exaggerate... we sometimes have to suppress the irritation we feel, which they would take to be what they're looking for... nostalgic admiration, envy...

But when we are not alone... when there's some poor, gawping dimwit with us in whom... faced with the Happiness flaunted in those clasping hands, those meeting eyes... something begins to stir...

He looks like a dog being teased with a lump of sugar, his eyes shine, his saliva dribbles, he jumps up, strains...

It's hard to put up with even for those of us who most of the time are absent-minded, indifferent... they can't stand it... They feel like protesting, intervening, stopping those hands that are creeping towards each other, intertwining, clasping... and shouting: Hands up!

But it's impossible to make a move. That would be enough to get us locked up. Such an attack on Happiness displaying itself in all its splendor, such a shameful assault... the victim herself, horrified by so much cynicism, ignoble incredulity...

It's true that it's among those victims that you find the truest believers, the real, faithful guardians of the cult.

And then we keep quiet.

Just once... when one of those offenders was parading in front of his victim—who was deprived of it—the Happiness of maternity, of paternity... when, growing more and more excited, uncontrolled, he was waving his flapping flag high in the air... we launched out, we went into the attack... "What Happiness? That's not Happiness!" "Not Happiness?" We were arrested, interrogated... "Isn't it happiness to have children? Could it by any chance be that yours haven't given you any?"

And at that, even the most audacious among us wavered... "I'm not saying that... but it seems to me that it also contains... well, it isn't always..." The victim looked at us with pity in her eyes...

Or with incredulity... she saw our effort... she refused to follow us...

Ah, those victims of "Happiness," there's really nothing to be done to help them.

Sometimes Happiness, trapped in a solid block in a book, hits a whole population... Modest, docile, peaceful people who up till then had managed by good-will to remain within the safety of recognized, intangible Happinesses, one fine day received this parcel bomb...

They had themselves brought it back from the bookshop or chosen it in a circulating library... and it exploded... a completely new Happiness created from unknown substances has blown to smithereens the thing that up till then had protected them, which they had cared for, preserved, and which they themselves and everyone around them had called Happiness... We saw poor people emerge from the debris looking distraught, lamenting... "So that's what it was... you see that load of rubbish... To think that we used to call that Happiness..." It's no use our trying to calm them down... "Oh yes, oh yes, it *was* Happiness, I assure you that you were living in it, you'll get it back..." "No. Never. Naturally we shall rebuild these premises, we shall go on living in them... what else could we do? But from now on we won't be able to call them Happiness, but a Cramped Life. Boredom. Prison. Penal servitude for life. Happiness is a long way from here... at the antipodes..."

In the face of the despair of these inhabitants of vast tracts of Happiness transformed into disaster areas, our lifesavers get busy... "It's not true, we know what it's made of, the 'Happiness' that has come and destroyed yours... we know it... Look..." and we display a series of images before their eyes, the way they do to cure drug addicts... They open their eyes wide, they protest... "But what's that? What are you showing us? Where's that total freedom here? That absence of all constraint? That perfect detachment? Those noble sentiments that no one has ever yet experienced? Those conversations through which we see beautiful, powerful, life-giving ideas circulating? No, you're trying to mislead us... you've invented that unbearable slavery, those jealousies, envies, meannesses, aggressivities... and those conversations that reveal so much conformism, so much boredom... We don't believe you, we believe the people who are living in it... they know what they're talking about... rather better than you do..." "Ah, they do indeed know better than we do, they know how to fool you... they take advantage of your humility... a humility... a credulity that knows no bounds... they want to force you to acknowledge their superiority... they're thirsting for domination, for conquests... they are not content with their self-adoration, they also want the whole world to see them as the only chosen ones, the only people worthy of possessing the one true Happiness..."

But these loud protests merely provoke knowing, ironic looks... And then nothing holds us back, no scruple, no respect for truth. We will stop at nothing to try to get the better of these destroyers, these killers... we hit out at them with any available means... with any wretched, low-down story, any humiliating and probably invented rebuff retailed by their vilest enemies...

And we are repulsed on all sides, driven out with disgust... we go home besmirched, with the words they have spat at us covering us, dripping... "Oh, you know, all those lies, that scandalmongering fabricated by envious people... The moment anyone superior succeeds... the ones who haven't his courage, his strength..."

That's where it sometimes leads us, this forgetfulness of what we owe to ourselves... this way of losing sight of ourselves... of giving ourselves recklessly...

Of giving ourselves body and soul... of forgetting that "Charity begins at home"...

But what sort of words have you just been using? You took them from outside, they aren't our sort of words, they aren't made for us...

What are you talking about here, among ourselves, what is that body you were talking of? What is that soul? And what is that "at home"?

What stain could find a place in our shifting immensity? What trace could it leave, that would last long enough to prevent us from starting again if a good opportunity arises...

"This lack of "self-awareness," this impossibility of knowing who we are, sometimes makes us go in for rather astonishing performances when we find ourselves face to face with one of those masterful personalities who herself knows only too well who she is...

Among all our feats of that sort there was one... perhaps the most splendid...

It must be admitted that we were helped by a particularly favorable combination of circumstances... We were on our own, closeted with one of those strong personalities...

One of the strongest we had ever met. Who "made herself felt," as they say... When she was there, as they also say, "no one else mattered"...

And she had invited us to spend a month's holiday alone with her.

Some of us here were surprised...

Some were flattered...

Those of you who are overcome with humility at every turn were in quite a state... What have we done to deserve this more than anyone else?... Will we be up to it?

From the moment we arrived you were filling us with doubt, anxiety... wasn't there... didn't we see a passing look on her face... of something like disappointment? regret?

We all began to tremble... Our committees met with all possible speed, conferred... there isn't a moment to lose... we must get one of our delegates to... Ah, but that's just it, which delegate? Whom did she want to invite? Whom does she want to meet? What is she expecting, hoping for?

And then, just as it is with a nervous candidate who hears the examiner asking him a question he wasn't expecting because it's so easy... what a relief! So that's what we have to give her to satisfy her curiosity, which, it must be said, is surprising in a person with a reputation for scorning everything practical, down-to-earth, petty.

But we were not at a loss to give her what she was looking for... Everything can be found in us... there are so many departments in us with so many products of all sorts...

We can supply on demand...

In the stocks, the reserves that as far as possible we usually avoid inspecting... if we get too close to them for too long, we get the impression that we're shrinking, stifling...

But that time, without the slightest repugnance, you began to search, and how zealously, how eagerly...

The thing is, as you well know, the moment we get involved in anything, no matter what, we always want to reach perfection... we're afraid we won't do everything within our power...

And there, when the stimulus we were given was so strong, and came from such a height...

You gave her even more than she was asking for... the representative you sent her supplied her with an abundance of...

Until the moment when the most vigilant of us, those of us who are the quickest to see the warning signs, observed something like a retreat... a contraction in her... was it the result of satiety? was it already disgust?

We call our delegate back... It would be better to keep still, to keep silent...

But we can't, we have to make amends at once, she has to be reconciled at all costs, to be made to relax... And without having received any further stimulus from her, without any new orders, we dart into the fray and give it to her at random, blindly...

Late that evening when we were alone, we conferred... You heard how she said she didn't like holidays... She must be pining, being so far away from her peers, even being so far away from those of her inferiors who are nevertheless capable of appreciating some of her qualities... But we, how can we see them? We haven't the resources... we don't possess the right knowledge. Which of us, incompetent as we are, could claim...?

Which of us! And you didn't say a word, you who are always persuading us that however ignorant we may be, no learned person... no "fount of knowledge" can exist who can have the impression when he's with us, whatever we may do, of being in unsuitable company, of demeaning himself... With us! Aren't we a world... worlds... in ourselves... beyond all comparison, all appreciation... But where were you, then?

You know very well that such strong personalities completely invade us... An occupying power that subjects us to its law... we can only obey its orders... All of us, we all of us looked for and brought back whatever we could find... Wouldn't that suit her? aren't these what might be called "interesting considerations," "original ideas," "new views," "amusing anecdotes," "fascinating accounts," "moving confessions"? We entrusted them to our delegates who succeeded one another, hastily pushed forward, abruptly pulled back, recalled...

When it happened that what we were offering was not accepted, when she rejected what we had put forward, we hurriedly took it back, we threw it on the scrap heap...

And there were even, it has to be admitted, *agents provocateurs* amongst us who were working for the oppressor and who by acts of deliberate imprudence...

They weren't deliberate... we'd been deprived of our willpower, hypnotized...

Yes, they *were* deliberate. You wanted to give that personality, whom our submission made increasingly capricious and demanding, an opportunity to snub us brutally, to attack us and take even more delight in her strength...

We may well wonder where we might have been led if we'd remained in her power long enough...

But even so, she had enough time to lead us quite far...

Yes, during that walk in the country... Who could forget it?... She's walking slowly with us down a path running along lucerne fields and meadows on one side and ripening corn on the other... When she stops, and we do the same, to contemplate, our representative keeps silent... and then we start off again and he begins to talk again, he holds forth, he expatiates... and for a few moments, without realizing it, we haven't been watching him quite so closely... his words come tumbling out one after the other...

We were all distracted by the colors, the scents, the sounds of wings, the birds abruptly taking flight... when all of a sudden... she let fall these words... "When the conversation descends to such a level"...

She murmured them as if she was talking to herself...

74

But she knew we could hear them... she pronounced them quite distinctly, on purpose...

And then we...

No, for pity's sake...

And then we didn't believe our ears...

That's right, we didn't believe them...

We chose not to have heard...

We felt supported by the imminence of our release... We left the next day. On the day and at the hour specified. We would never have dared bring this moment forward...

When, after leaning out of the window of the train and waving "a last farewell," we go into the compartment, we are once again among free people, worthy people, people like us, as we immediately become again... Words flit between them and us, brush against us... the innocent names of the places we're going to, we're coming from... visit to the farm of old relations, business, holiday with a friend at the seaside... Ah yes, I know it, it's a beautiful place...

If we had spoken to them about the other place, the one we'd come away from...

But it has no name. It's situated in regions whose existence these people are unaware of... If we had described that month spent in captivity...

If we had told them that we had been invaded, driven into abject submission by the implacable power of an enormous occupying force... imagine their surprise, their incredulity, their suspicion...

We can hardly believe it ourselves, we've already stopped thinking about it, we haven't the slightest wish to.

But a little later, when she intimated to us that she was hoping to see us again soon...

Then the same wave of repulsion swept over us all, no, it's not possible we haven't the time, not a moment, we have so much work to do... A surge of renewed life...

But above all the certainty that she was still far away, that we were out of her reach, enabled us to take such an elevated stand, to dare to refuse because of our work!

Because of "our important work"... we even raised ourselves to that level...

But she... how was it possible? she wasn't in the least surprised, or shocked, by such presumptuousness...

We heard that she told anyone prepared to listen that she had spent a delightful, unforgettable month with us...

Everywhere she went she was profuse in her praise of our personality... She had rarely met anyone so sensitive, tolerant, well-balanced, intelligent... in short, the most staggering things we could possibly hear...

So that was the person we had been. The person she had invited. The person she had entertained. The companion she had perceived... true to himself and worthy of her...

So *that* was the construction she had seen before her, which had prevented her from seeing our tumultuous mass...

An edifice that she had certainly not erected herself... otherwise after a month we would finally have eroded it, damaged it, we would even have demolished it...

It had to be a monument that was as solid as a rock. Built of strong materials. Maybe by people she was sure were "competent."

What can it look like, this monument?

What's the use of wasting our time? We all know very well that we shall never see it, we've always been incapable of seeing even its vaguest outlines.

What got into us, that time, what completely occupied us, what swept everything else in us aside, were the words of an old poem...

An old poem we once learned, which disappeared long ago...

It suddenly invaded us, it flowed through us, it poured out of our mouth...

We were it, and it alone... Our voice was its voice... all its inflections came from it... it made our voice fall gently at the end of each rhyme... stop just a little... just long enough for its vibrations to be prolonged... then it made it rise again, start again, remain suspended...

Float for a moment on the limpid, emerald water, above the clear depths...

When its last word had been uttered, when its resonances were finally lost in the distance, we suddenly came back to ourselves...

The awakening of the Sleeping Beauty...

Don't try to mock us after the event... We were all surprised...

We found ourselves standing on a terrace, surrounded by people...

Friends who had seen one of their number suddenly stand up, recite a poem... They'd listened to it...

Every word had come out and filled the surrounding space that belonged to them as it did to us...

None of them would have believed us if we had sworn that we had become oblivious of their presence...

That we had become oblivious of ourselves...

There wasn't the slightest image of ourselves in us... not the vaguest picture of our silhouette standing there on the terrace in their midst... Head high, arm outstretched... Reciting in a vibrant voice...

Obviously... how could they doubt it?... so that the words would carry to them better... So that the words would reach them, enter into them...

And they received them... they retained... detained them... they examined them, it's a poem they are very familiar with, they too learnt it at school...

They know its standing... which isn't of the highest... It's one of those poems we sometimes see in rather bad company... among the *déclassé*... in rather third-rate anthologies... It isn't of very noble origin... Its author isn't one of the greatest... He's one of the modest ones, who aren't lacking in talent, though... "But actually, that particular poem isn't one that I personally... Do you really like it so much?"

Then we start our tug of war... You make a dash, we hold you back, we hang on to you... Don't do that, leave it alone, don't try to take it back, to defend it... You struggle... But we can't possibly leave it in the hands of that brute... You can see very well what he's doing to it... he's already tearing it to pieces... he's pulled that word out, he's grabbed it, he's holding it in his hand, he's turning it over, he's presenting it to us... "Do you like this word?"... We implore you... Leave it with him... Don't try to rescue it, it's bloodless, already dead, that word displayed there all alone, cut off from the others...

80

All we achieve is that you agree to send out some-one who, without touching any of the words, manages to say in a cold voice, an aloof tone, as aloof as possi-ble... "Well, personally, it so happens that I rather like that poem... As for explaining why... That isn't the way to judge a text, by examining one word, and then an-other, picked out here or there, detached from the rest..."

But there's no way of holding you back com-pletely... before we go home, in your strangulated voice you let fall a few trembling droplets... "I have to say that for me that poem... it contains true innocence... some-thing intact... which moves me..."

And then, pulled very hard by us, you retreat, you allow yourselves to be shut away with us... But you're still very agitated... calm down... stop worrying, they've already dropped that poem, they've dismissed it, it doesn't deserve so much attention from them, they've let it go and join the others of its rank which they don't frequent, they won't go near it any more...

They may, though, but only because it will still be associated with us, our distinctive sign... our orna-ment... Because they'll never obliterate *us*. They'll never let go of that lovely present they've received... that unexpected gift...

That trump card they'll hold when they play their favorite game, the portraits game...

When they're lucky enough that on that day, the person whose portrait people are painting, will be us.

What a surprise they'll cause when they produce us... "Yes, it's barely believable... Who would ever have been able to imagine it? He, so reserved... so reticent... I might even say secretive... He suddenly stood up in the middle of the terrace... facing the sea, at sunset... he seemed elated..."

You can just see the people around him dancing up and down, clapping their hands... "It's not possible!" "Yes yes, head high, arm stretched up to the horizon... Reciting a poem..." "A poem? In front of you?" "Reciting isn't the word, declaiming, rather..." "Oh no! Did he really?... What poem?" "A nondescript poem... of the most mediocre sort... the sort... you know... that we all learned at junior school..." "But I've known him to be so exigent... I thought he was so particular..." "Yes, too finicky, even..." "He's sometimes so disparaging about the greatest..." "That's what happens, isn't it, with these aesthetes... When all of a sudden their true preferences come to light, you're dumbfounded..." "Yes, you can see everything they've repressed coming to the surface and being exposed..." "Did he want to force it on you? He's quite a tyrant, you know... When you don't share his tastes he can fly into a rage..." "No, that time he kept cool... Only, when one of us expressed a few reservations, he turned pale, he protested gently... his voice trembled a little..." "I must admit that you amaze me... I see him as someone who is not exactly what they call 'poetically-minded'... But who is oriented towards everything that is most 'practical'... When I need precise information on some very 'down-to-earth' subjects, I ask him... I get the feeling that he's pleased... that's his element..."

Bravo! You, who sometimes manage so well to mix with other people, it seems as if you've really done your best this time... Anyone might think we were playing their game...

With one reservation, though... the fact that they credited us with such a well-developed practical sense... that they saw it as one of our main characteristics...

Don't you remember what happened, though, when we succumbed to the influence of that powerful personality? Our efforts to be useful to her? Our zeal?... We rushed around, searching our stocks, our reserves... to bring her... to satisfy her demand... we even anticipated... Nothing was too petty...

So she really was the one you finally got to talk?

Yes, we can hear her... And you know, it may very well still happen that she takes possession of us, and that that same eagerness comes over us again...

No. There's one thing we can be quite sure of, which is that that will never again happen to us.

"Never again" are words that we ought not to use... With us, there's nothing we can ever really swear to... It isn't impossible that one fine day we shall fall into her hands again...

And it isn't impossible that, after our performance at sunset on the terrace, she would say to us: "You know what I've been told? That you like poetry... that you know a whole lot of poems by heart... that you recite them..." And she'll nod her head with an air of approval...

Oh no, why pile it on? Why pile on those airs of approval, those movements of the head? It's implausible, it's extravagant... words pronounced in a tone that's a little... slightly... surprised... they'll do...

That's right. That's all. How right that sounds... Doesn't it seem to you that we've already heard them, those words?

"What he said wounded me. Yes, I was upset. Why exactly? Oh, I don't really know. What's certain is that I found it unpleasant."

Now there's a way of speaking that's instantly recognizable...

That's the way someone who loves himself speaks to himself...

Yes, we here, among ourselves... we don't use those words, "me," "I"...

Or rather let's say we don't use them any longer... We still did, after that "You don't love yourself" hit us and caused such a great upheaval in us, when we realized more clearly than ever that we had broken up into a multitude of disparate "I's"... whom could we love in all that? For a time, several "I's," "me's," "you's" were still questioning each other within us: "How could you have done that?"...

And then these "I's," these "me's," these "you's" disappeared...

When, exactly?

We didn't really notice... it was as if they became naturally diluted into shapeless masses... several "we's," several "you's"... made up of many similar elements...

Like banks of fish of the same species, flights of birds moving as one, groups whose members have the same tendencies... To talk about them in the singular... no, we couldn't do that any more... we needed a "we," a collective "you."

It's only the spokesmen we still send to the outside world who go on using those "I's," those "me's."

But they have to, otherwise how would they manage to make themselves heard?

86

But let's come back to that "I was upset. Yes, it wounded me."

There is, as you realize, something exciting, promising, in them, in those words that someone who loves himself says to himself. They may be a gift from heaven, those words that suddenly occurred to us... "I was upset. He wounded me. I found it unpleasant."

He says it with such conviction. It's a statement of fact.

Let's see how he reacts.

Well, according to his character, his temperament... which anyway he is familiar with. Which he's fond of talking about... "Personally, you know, I'm always flying off the handle," he gets carried away, he flares up, he too uses wounding words... Or else, if he is as he claims "one of those people who think that 'Revenge is a dish that should be eaten cold,'" the insolent fellow "has got it coming to him," one day he'll give him "a dose of his own medicine"... Or else, he's of a conciliatory nature... "I detest trouble-making, cutting remarks, quarrels... I ignore them... And anyway, unless they're very serious, I forget them..." Or else... "I prefer not to see unpleasantness. I'd rather tell myself: he knows not what he does..." Or again... "I've always liked to forgive... Ever since I was very small,

87

ever since my mother made me say my prayers every evening... Forgive us our trespasses as we forgive them that trespass against us..."

Well, each of these privileged people reacts directly in accordance with what he is...

So do we, sometimes our body reacts immediately, our face blushes or pales...

But afterwards, what a difference between the person who loves himself and ourselves... What an upheaval in us, what agitation... what exactly has happened? What made us so suddenly become red in the face? And what made us flinch?

And you immediately reply... in such cases you're always the first to reply... "There was something wounding in what he said to us..."

But as this response lacks assurance, dignity, an air of outraged majesty... there's a tremor in it... its tone is almost embarrassed... guilty... or else aggressive... it looks as if you're trying to defend yourself...

Inevitably. We know very well that we are the most fragile here, the most delicate... It sometimes takes so little to shake us... That's why we're always suspect... our shudders, our withdrawals, are examined with suspicion...

88

Don't forget that allowing ourselves to be carried along by you has cost us some rebuffs... Your vulnerability, when we've allowed it to contaminate us, to show itself to the outside world, has got us called some very disagreeable names...

Paranoid. Persecuted.

Or at best hypersensitive. Very touchy.

And yet we had to listen to you. There are some wounding words that one can't pretend not to hear without incurring other dangers...

Without getting oneself called other names, all just as unflattering...

We must get the majority of us together, to examine...

The thing is that we never all manage to get together at the same time... some of us are always thinking of other things, with "our heads in the clouds"...

Or apathetic... Lazy... Dozing... To manage to wake them up... And there are others...

But what's the use of trying to collect them? There are so many of all sorts... we have no time to lose...

Words arriving from outside have wounded those of us who are usually the most sensitive... Ah, you too?... Even you? You felt?...

Yes, we who are nevertheless not what might be called touchy...

It's true that your lack of touchiness has sometimes induced us, when we've been following your lead, to "stomach" things that...

It makes us blush, now, just the very thought...

Well, this time we have discovered what was so insolent in those words...

A desire to wound?

That's not so sure...

But it's likely...

But likely isn't enough... for us it must be certain.

It *is,* more or less... but to avoid any misunderstanding, let's just call it thoughtlessness... a lack of concern about the effect those words might produce... a lack of respect for "our person"...

90

Allow us, so as to avoid... you know how distressing it is to make rash accusations...

One regrets it so much, later...

Even if it was merely one of those "gaffes" th:
escape you, you'd like to take it back...

Oh no, it wasn't that.

Is that so sure?

Absolutely. The words were chosen and utter
deliberately... and in any case without the slightest co
cern... whether they wound us or not, what does it m:
ter... one wants to say them and one allows oneself

People allow themselves with us. Because with u
everything is allowable... Look at them, the ones wl
are drowsing or daydreaming... nothing bores them
much as these examinations, these deliberations... S
how they're waking up... With us? Really? With us, pe
ple can allow themselves...? You'd think a mosquito h
stung them, they shake themselves, they scratch the
selves...

Impossible to act as if nothing has happened... \
must make up our minds...

It's a bit late... The reply should have come immediately...

Where were you, though? You hardly noticed... you wake up now...

You can't count on us, as you well know... we're busy elsewhere, we have better things to do... it's up to you to defend us...

Now, over there, what do we look like?

We can still put it right...

You must be joking! Put it right!... You and your after-wit...

We can find an opportunity...

No, no and no... we don't want anything to do with those retaliations, those regurgitations, that cold revenge... we can't stand them... we're the ones they humiliate, they degrade us all.

And then, are we really convinced? Is there really any reason to deal severely...?

And are those words really worth preserving here, among people who keep things of the sort...

A repository from which they sometimes resurface...

Where we can find them if we need them...

Isn't it better to try to destroy them? to wash away, to rub out their traces?

Don't forget your fear of action... your laziness... whatever you do, don't move. Play the ostrich...

We ought to... we need to... we need to hear them again... to repeat them in the same tone of voice... Listen carefully...

It's true that they contain... we didn't really notice it at the time... those words contain something...

We feel diminished, crushed...

Not we. Really not. They're nothing. Light-hearted words...

Idle talk...

Idle? No, not idle... we have to see where those words come from... perhaps from bitterness? from hidden suffering?

What qualms if we wounded someone who was already wounded! Let's throw all that on the scrap heap, then... let's forget about it...

Oh you, our saints and martyrs... you'll never manage to get us to turn the other cheek... Because one day we shall have to...

That's for sure. Once a thief, always a thief. God knows what new impulse will drive that embittered unfortunate to...

Against us... we're the obvious target...

Yes, with us, why hold back? Where is a better outlet to be found? Ah, here they are, returning in force... A wave of heat rises... How could we have agreed?...

But we don't agree. At the first opportunity...

Or even before... a chill, a distance... He won't know what's hit him...

Wait a moment... you have no right...

What will they think of us? For such a trifle? But they'll say...

Oh, that's enough, we'll never see an end to it. Such a lack of cohesion, such an absence of discipline... of central power...

There's only one way... send a messenger...

To make inquiries of one of the people who are lucky enough to know who they are.

And that "who" has a government. A code of laws.

He knows what words addressed to him and in what sort of tone of voice constitute legitimate grounds for taking legal action. Deserve punishment. He knows it right away, he doesn't need to ask himself any questions.

He can distinguish in the twinkling of an eye between what can or cannot be done to him.

Go and ask him... Make sure you tell him... Without distorting anything, otherwise what use would his answer be?

It'll be difficult... I don't dare...

But you must, we shall be there, behind you...

That one, now, seems an obvious choice. Compact. Solid. Clear-cut outlines. And it's quite obvious that a circle has been drawn around him...

By himself, naturally.

Those are the limits he won't allow anyone to go beyond. Placed at the correct distance.

The one he thinks is correct.

The one he knows is correct. Beyond a doubt.

He's the one we need. Come on, don't hesitate...

You—our "I" that we can't see... but your face is probably now showing the expression of sincerity, of gravity, of someone who wants to know the truth... "Would you have considered those words offensive?..."

Speak to him, ask... This is the moment, don't let the chance go by...

There we are, then. So we weren't wrong, we the hypersensitive ones, the touchy ones, we are satisfied... we've got our nerve back. We couldn't have asked for anything better: "Of course those words were wounding. Inadmissible. So insolent..." And this, accompanied by an air of surprise, of indignation...

But now we feel really wounded... the wound is becoming deeper... enlarged... it hurts... Can't we try to get another answer?

Why be content with that one?

Oh, you! With you, we shall never come to the end of it... How many more inquiries, opinion polls do you need?

Just one more attempt... Just ask the same question once more... To that one... he'll suit us equally well, he too has all the requisite qualities... He's looking at you sympathetically, and he's alone in front of you...

No, there's another presence...

But as if in the background... very shadowy... Take no notice of it, start... very simply... "Look, I'm going to surprise you... but I'd like you to tell me..."

What happened? How did it suddenly come...?

It was so abrupt, brutal... an assault of such violence...

Let's try and get over it now... it was a great shock...

Quick, our usual tranquillizer... our only remedy... Look at it all again from the beginning...

Why from the beginning? Only from the moment when you asked him: "What do you think about it? Were those words wounding?" He looks surprised, shocked... "But of course they were. They were extremely impertinent... It takes some nerve..." And then the conversation continues...

Exchanges of remarks of utter banality... about anything and everything... just "rabbiting on"...

We were getting bored, we were going to call you back... when suddenly, really "without rhyme or reason"...

After your remark... which couldn't have been more innocuous... We were barely listening to you, and he too seemed far away...

But during that time, in him... Look, we can see it so clearly...

Yes... and we are starting to calm down...

We are even feeling pleased... Look at that turbulence seething in him... accumulated over the course of the days... and rekindled at this moment by boredom...

We can act quickly, it's all so obvious... It's rising in him, irritation, exasperation...

And there, the outlet is all ready... we've just shown it to him... No protection here, no alarm signal, no one is running the slightest risk... Look at what's being allowed... with impunity...

What's being allowed? Someone else has allowed himself? Then why not me?

And by him... we'd lost sight of it... that shadowy presence... shadowy but stimulating... a witness whom he is going to show just how far *he* can allow himself...

His safety valve opens wide... releases, pours out...

We must hurry, it's too easy, we're getting bored...

Still nothing else appearing... only that movement... that reaction... the predator that has sensed its palpitating, hesitating prey within its reach... "I don't know... you must help me... was it really offensive?"

That's enough now, that'll do.

Perhaps there are still some here who aren't certain, who would like to ask yet another person, one of those who know, whether what hit you full in the face was real spittle?

If, when he let out that roar, put his heavy paw down on you, stuck his claws into you, it was really wounding?

No? No need for further opinion polls?

We are all convinced.

That's the very least...

All united. What discipline. What orderliness.

All subject to a mighty central power.

Which is going to direct our actions...

Defensive? Attacking?

That'll depend... Our government knows what it is advisable to do in each case to prevent us from suffering similar assaults in future.

But you know, this omnipotent central power... This invulnerability protected by an inviolable defense mechanism... well-guarded frontiers...

All of us welded together in a solid block...

A "Me"... That's what we can call it...

Yes, "Me"... Can it be possible?... Can I dare? Can I ask myself that question? ask myself where the difference lies between someone who loves himself and me?

What power... What independence...

I don't doubt it, me, yes, me, I too love myself.

But what is it that's beginning to stir? What is that disturbance hiding in the corners, what are those little giggles?

Guffaws... can you see what is amusing them, what they find so funny? They're drawing caricatures, grotesque, clownish pictures... that elongated neck, those slightly bulging eyes, straining... questioning, waiting... lips pushed out, encircled by the words: "Don't you think... I don't know... this is what I was told, this is in what circumstances... what's your opinion of it? was it wounding?"

Can you hear those whispers?... It takes someone very stupid... not to be able to judge people... to go and ask that person... Yet it was so obvious... But we're so gullible...

This time laughter bursts out on all sides, spreads, we're shaking with laughter... The most comic thing was first of all our surprise... What's happened to us? How did he dare? Why? We're priceless...

And then, when we have understood... our satisfaction, our swashbuckling assurance... Let him try, then, let him start again... he'll see what stuff I'm made of...

"I," "I'm"... Just look at that...

But that's not all: I love myself.

Once again we have dared go as far as that.

———

How is it that we have never yet tried to see what may be happening in us when all of a sudden... it's surprising... unexpected, even for us all... without the slightest reason we go so far as to call down on our head what anyone else...

Anyone else, that's saying a lot... let's rather say someone who wants to protect himself just a little, who loves himself however little... such a person would obviously ward off, thrust aside...

But we, we invite threats, we provoke danger...

It looks as if we rush headlong towards it...

Even so we ought to make an effort... to try to see...
To choose an example...

What example? There are so many...

Why don't we take this one, which is still recent...
It hasn't yet been broken up into scattered fragments
that have to be put back end to end... We can still see
them in their proper order...

To start with, a few people sitting in a circle, talking...

What about, exactly?

One can only make out the pleasant, lively sound
of their voices... It's a gathering of friends, of acquaintances who are joined together by the solidly, prudently-
woven thread of a quiet conversation.

Nothing that sticks out. Nothing that stings.

Our delegate...

Your delegate...

But we had all accepted him. He's always the one
we allow to represent us in such circumstances...

104

The one who, in the presence of any group of people, begins to resemble them. They rub off on him...

He immediately allows himself "to be cut to the same pattern"...

Precisely because he is your emanation, you who adapt so well... you begin to feel nothing, to think nothing other than what the people around you feel, think...

So much so that you sometimes arouse in them... Is it disdain?

Don't let's digress. Forget us. Let's rather admire our delegate... how well he fulfills his function... how well he knows how to make the conversation with the others run smoothly... how to give it a gentle nudge when its pace slackens... how to extricate it when for a moment it gets stuck in silence...

And that's when there appears in us...

Where from? Why?

How can we know?... What doesn't come to our mind? So many unexpected images, ridiculous scenes, crop up in us when we are there, in the background, idle, relaxed, only half-listening to the insipid remarks being exchanged...

It suddenly arose... We didn't invite it...

No, you see, it came of its own accord without warning, and it remains there without moving, it digs in... a wet pavement glistening in the sunlight, lined with chestnut trees in blossom, café terraces with their awnings down... and that massive figure advancing... that broad, artless, smiling face, that candid gaze and that big warm voice... "Ah, it's you, how are you?" And that big hand being held out and our hand also being held out and allowing itself to be grasped and shaken... which itself shakes that hand...

Quite firmly...

Yes, as firmly as it is shaken...

All the same, though... let's look carefully... can't we see, at the moment when our hand in its turn... well, just before it's held out... a few movements of hesitation... the hint of a pullback...

Of course, there *is* one... But you know very well that nothing can stop our hand, make it hang limply from our lowered arm, conceal itself behind our back when another hand, no matter whose, is held out towards it, ready to shake it... When has it ever happened that we refused to let it be "polluted"?

But while the conversation over there is continuing, let us rather look at the image that is still here, in the background, becoming clearer, more vivid, we haven't dismissed it, we aren't trying to find another to put in its place...

It's becoming more and more animated, it's becoming more prominent, it wants to come out, to show itself off... in a moment it's going to lash out with some words...

We can already hear the strident cries of our oracles announcing disaster...

A state of disorder, of disarray can be seen in us...

A free-for-all between those who would like to repel that image, smash it, and those who accept it, who want it to show itself...

Between the poltroons, the shamefaced, the proud, the courageous, the guilty who long for confession, for expiation, the people who take refuge in secrecy, the ones who have a taste for martyrdom, the ones who fear nothing so much as suffering...

It's strange, but we can't see anything of all that... you must be dreaming...

You're taking a census of the population, here, as it usually appears in the lists...

You don't dare depart from the familiar, the plausible...

And that is precisely what we are seeing here is *not*... No trace here of disarray, no battle... with surprising rapidity the image propels, shoots out the words... they get engulfed in us, they traverse us, we are an empty, open space, nothing rises up in revolt as they pass, they push our delegate out of the way and, through the mouth of the spokesman they have chosen to replace him, they come out with...

To start with, a very powerful first word, the name that adheres to the massive body with the nice candid face so that he can introduce himself to all the assembled company... his family name: Galion...

Yes, Galion. This name abruptly severs the solidly-woven thread of the conversation...

And other words arrive through this rupture... "I met him the other day... He was surprised to see me again... it had been so long... He came up to me holding out his hand... He looked so..." As one man, the silent group breathes: "Galion? And you shook his hand?... Oh come, you know very well he's a swine... dangerous..." Now voices come from all sides... "It's because of people like him..." "You shook Galion's hand!" The voices become more and more vibrant... "Excuse me, but no, that I cannot... It's an insult to us all... to everyone who has... whom he has..." And then silence...

If we had bodies, faces, we could see ourselves as a jostling throng, crowding together, stretching our necks to see what's happening over there, among them, what they're doing with us now...

And in our eyes, on our lips, there'd be an expression...

Yes... Curious as it might seem... of contentment... the words we allowed to traverse us and fall into them have produced the effect that was to be expected...

It's a sort of satisfaction like that produced by a chemical operation when the reagent poured on has acted according to rule. No mistake. Everything is in order.

It's also the relief one can feel when the ineluctable has finally been accomplished.

It's the serenity that comes through submission to fate.

109

We are the interested onlookers at our own execution...

Our own execution? Whatever are you saying? You're talking like them...

You're forgetting that what they take for a real execution can only be what in the old days was an execution in effigy...

They're fussing around what the words we provided them with have enabled them to fabricate...

Around that doll... that dummy they constructed in the image of what we made appear in front of them...

They exhibit it with an ignominious label attached to it... They throw it into the communal grave where they bury cowards, traitors, enemies...

As for us... and that's also where our detachment, our contentment comes from, *we* are still here, observing them...

They can do nothing against *us*...

There's no way of getting the better of *us*...

$\mathbf{B}$ut what happens when we aren't the ones who have provided the materials they have used to fabricate us?

How far away we are from that relief, that odd contentment, when our envoy is talking with someone from outside and exchanging words stemming from our common concerns... at least that's what we think... and when we realize that something is emanating from the other... seeping out of his face, his gaze... something that was certainly not produced in him by the object of the conversation...

He can see it, that object, but at a certain distance...

Clearly enough to be able to talk about it, but he's concentrating for all he's worth on the person he's talking to... On the person who's saying "I"...

Whom we have made our delegate for our dealings with him and whose sole function is to convey to him the reflections, convictions, information, and questions of those of us here who are concerned with the object of the conversation...

It isn't "I" he sees... it's someone else, but whom?

Someone he himself has fabricated...

With what? What materials? Where did he get them from?

Like people whose house has been burgled, we search in ourselves, we look everywhere... Perhaps they were things that were in us but which we hadn't seen... We never make an inventory...

How could we, in this immense jumble, this accumulation, this disorder?

He may have felt a movement insinuating itself into us which revealed itself to the outside world by a word, an intonation, a frown, pursed lips...

And he has frozen that movement, he's detached it, preserved it, labelled it, he's found a name for it. The name people give to a certain trait of character...

Perhaps he's added some more traits to it...

Just one might perhaps have been enough for him... one of those nuclei around which a whole personality is constructed...

A personality which is not the one that ought to be attributed to our delegate...

Our ambassador has presented credentials which have been refused...

No, nothing so brutal. They have been duly accepted, but he is regarded with suspicion, he's placed under surveillance...

It's strange, there's no visible sign of it... We feel it, that's all.

The words we send over there, to the other, reach him, just touch him, bounce off...

What does manage to penetrate him is something different, which seeps out of us...

Our groups become flustered... you aren't the ones who should have sent a delegate... what he says lacks conviction, persuasion, it must look like indecision, spinelessness... we must recall him...

Replace him by our own, one who comes from the most convinced, the most passionate among us... the object of the conversation will become closer, denser, the other will become full of it, he'll stop observing us...

But it could be that such strength of conviction, of passion, attracts him even more towards the person speaking... He calmly examines his excitation, his trepidation...

We must look elsewhere, there's no time to lose...

This too-passionate "I" withdraws, abandoning the object of the conversation... We must hurry, whatever happens we mustn't let a silence become established...

We quickly replace this "I" by a frivolous, lighthearted "I"... After a pause marked by a sigh, our new "I" comes out with... "Ah, that isn't everything. We

114

shouldn't get excited... in any case, no matter what we think, no matter what we do..." and he throws a delightfully inconsequential object into the conversation... it flutters in front of the other, his eyes follow it vaguely, but you feel he isn't relaxing his vigilance... he's still closely observing the person talking to him...

Right, we withdraw this envoy, we present an "I" who shows that he has his feet firmly on the ground, that he possesses common sense, a clear mind, he himself says so: "I'm a realist... People sometimes accuse me of cynicism..." but however powerful, weighty, scathing his words may be, they don't manage to penetrate the other so far as to hold his attention, to distract him from what he sees...

We don't become discouraged... the procession of delegates continues...

What's the good of quoting all their remarks?... There are some of all sorts...

Some visibly amuse him... boastful, lying, scandal-mongering... more and more awkward, pathetic, as our resources run dry...

Those of our last sallies... Of our last desperate attempts...

It's obvious that he's not allowing himself to be distracted. Nothing can efface the person he has never stopped seeing in front of him... Impossible to tell who...

Someone who looks like us, who bears our name, who answers to the same description, is taken for us, charged, arrested and imprisoned...

Entirely in the power of his one and only jailer... Given a life sentence...

No, that's where the comparison stops. It's a prison we can escape from... Never go near again...

We're already moving away from it, from that prison and its warder... It would take a big effort to return to that vicinity...

We're recovering our transparency... other people's looks go through us...

The words we think suitable to send into them are received in the right way by them, they examine them, they don't allow themselves to be distracted by them... Our spokesman doesn't hold... or in any case no more than is advisable... their attention...

So here we are, once again wearing our precious cap...

The magic cap that makes people invisible in fairy stories.

What is it that suddenly... like a doubt... a sense of frustration...

Ah, your scruples again... we felt so good, away from our prison... wearing our cap...

But would we have been so keen to regain our invisibility if we had felt that the other's steady gaze on the "I" we were presenting to him exuded admiration, delight, love...

Love? Right, but in that case a love that isn't mutual... because a mutual love would lead us...

Elsewhere... God knows where... Somewhere we shall certainly have to try to go one day...

For the moment, while our "I" goes on talking about the object we're concerned with, we feel a warmth, such a gentle light, flowing out of the person he's talking to and spreading over us...

And some of us can bear it no longer... they wallow in it, indulge in it... For them too the object of the conversation becomes remote...

They're too fascinated by the image that the other is obviously contemplating... it must be admirable, captivating... it can't be the image of our delegate... it's clearly that of someone the other has fabricated and put in his place...

But once again, fabricated from what? What has he found?

Vain as you are, you others, how you would like to resemble that image!... and even make it more charming...

Only what on earth can it resemble? You search, you go through our collections which preserve the expressions of people who are admired, unreservedly adored, which we have taken from their portraits, their photographs, their faces seen on our television screens...

You choose a profound, hallucinated look... staring into faraway places that no other look can reach... lips with the bitter curl that comes from the vision of our tragic condition...

We feel that you're injecting that same haunted air into our eyes... you're giving our lips that same disenchanted expression... or else that sad, tender smile...

We could never make an end of the list of everything you could choose from our collections...

For a few moments, helpless, we watch your efforts...

We're afraid that however blinded he may be, the other will notice your ploys...

You humiliate us...

We become more and more bored during the course of this exchange of words in which our opinions, our questions are blurred, blunted, relegated to the background... In the end we manage to come back to the object... we cling on to it, we press it, we squeeze words out of it that must penetrate over there, into the other... he'll be forced to concentrate his whole attention on the object, to observe it from very close to, he'll lose sight of us...

But our words that are so full of conviction only manage to reach him through the image of us that he is still contemplating... They come out of it in such a way as to make him smile delightedly, nod several times, clearly intimating his unconditional agreement, his admiration...

We try to come out with more subversive, shocking arguments, their violence will shatter that screen and they'll penetrate him intact, coming straight out of the object...

But the other is still looking at us with his approving, tender gaze... It's quite clear that he is enchanted by the person he sees in the place of our spokesman... everything this enchanter says delights him... so much courage, intransigence, originality, such a pure passion.

And now we are trapped, this time in one of those golden cages, grand hotels, transatlantic liners, de luxe sanitoria... ourselves a luxury item, preserved, tidied up, cleaned up, dusted off, polished...

You can bear it no longer, you suddenly burst out of the place into which you've been relegated, restricted, you're going to blow everything up... You make an idiotic expression appear on our face, you pour inept words, vulgar laughs out of our mouth...

In vain... this time too we can only find our salvation in flight...

Put ourselves at the greatest possible distance... Get back into our element... in which we have the impression that for the other, outside, we are like the air that surrounds him...

That his gaze passes through us without seeing us.

What's the use of waiting, of putting it off... we know very well that we'll have to come to it eventually, to what is called "mutual love"...

When they came and told us that what we were experiencing was "mutual love," it disturbed us, embarrassed us... What was it they saw, then? What could those words be applied to?

And yet we hadn't gone outside to erect and show off one of those magnificent constructions...

And anyway, even if we'd tried, we wouldn't have found the components that could have made it prestigious, admirable...

We'd stayed by ourselves...

We had the impression we usually have, of being invisible...

Invisible to ourselves, too...

As if we were alone amongst ourselves... as if there was no one else here with us...

And in actual fact we *were* alone... there was no one here with us but us...

Perhaps... one day... the disappearance...

But how can something that is an inseparable part of us disappear without us disappearing ourselves?

Death might come and snatch it...

That's when what manages to survive, while the part that has been removed is vanishing, notices... but what?... What was it?

126

It would seem that our enormous, shifting mass had increased even more... was denser, more vibrant... it spread out, it covered vaster spaces, it hemmed them in more closely, it stuck to them more tightly...

But all that as if going without saying...

As our existence goes without saying... When we're in good health, do we notice our breathing, the movement of our blood, the play of our muscles?

Yet there were moments...

Seen from outside, they would have seemed unimportant...

When something... how to describe it?...

Was it a color, a line, a barely perceptible nuance, an intonation, a silence... but that can't let itself...

That could never be captured by any word...

It opened out, dug a path in us through the same substance, returned to the same source...

What source?

Wasn't it Cézanne who said, apropos of something else...

But was it really something else he was talking about when he said that "it is embedded in the very roots of being... In the intangible source of feeling"?

As for feeling, that is where words circulate, alight, designate...

It was amusing to go on a little excursion there from time to time...

One part of ourselves broke loose, went outside, put on its best clothes for the occasion, those of two quite different people.

There, we found the words put at our disposal, and we came out with them: "I love you"...

Let's imagine this: an autonomous "I" presents himself to a "You" and utters the word "love"... That "I" can also ask for it back... "Do you love me?"

It's curious. When we were using those expressions: "I love you," "Do you love me?" we were a little surprised that we couldn't keep a straight face, we felt a smile appearing in our eyes, on our lips...

It must have come from the confused impression we had that we were children playing...

That's right, children amusing themselves by imitating the grown-ups.

We could also play at portraits. The "I" placing himself at a distance and observing the "You"... Isolating what appears here or there, collecting it up, describing it... "You know what you are? You're goodness personified. Who is more generous than you?"... And to make it funnier, placing himself at an even greater distance... "You have such charm..."

"I" could also paint a completely different portrait of "You"... "You want me to tell you what you are? You're selfish. I don't know anyone more petty... more spiteful than you. I don't love you. I hate you."

We could provoke each other, fight, all the time feeling that it isn't serious, it isn't in earnest...

Schoolchildren fooling around in the playground.

We amused ourselves like that now and again and then we mixed it all up, all the words we had played with, the way you shuffle dice, counters, cards, and put them away higgledy-piggledy until the next time...

But it happened... you remember that time, when suddenly, just when we were going to change out of our best clothes and become ourselves again, "You" moved even further away from "I," went off, "You" went and joined the people over there, mingled with them like someone who had always lived among them, who had always been one of them...

Entirely different from "I." A stranger who felt perfectly at home...

There he is, leaning back in his armchair, crossing his legs, waggling his foot self-confidently, and coming out with the sort of words they use...

Uncouth, mass-produced words, brutally grabbing, grasping, crushing just the very thing in us that escapes them, the thing they can't approach, the thing they daren't touch...

Taking possession of what belongs to us alone, holding it out to them... "You see, it happened that in one of those special moments I had the feeling of being... how can I put it..." he's going to hand it over to them, let them examine it, he's going to submit it to them...

In another moment, between us, there will be a permanent separation...

Between us, the only kind of separation where no reconciliation is possible.

But he says nothing, he shuts his eyes... it's there in him, intact... he rejects the words that might touch it... He comes back to us...

So it was just a joke...

Our mischievous little imps had got hold of him, they'd made him carry the game too far...

But how could we have believed that he wasn't playing, that he had really become one of them?

After that bad dream, how wonderful to be back amongst ourselves again...

It's so good to be together again, to merge, to melt...

Everything is coming back to life, quivering... something intangible protected by silence is passing through the same substance in us, returning to the same source...

And so we had to know: what was it, then, that they noticed in us, that they immediately recognized and called "mutual love"?

We never know how far you'll go when you're motivated by that sort of curiosity...

If we hadn't stopped you, God knows what you would have gone and told them about these games between us, about our lightheartedness...

No, even so not that, we'd never have gone that far... and anyway, they wouldn't have understood a thing.

The only thing they'd have noticed is that we didn't feel what can be called "mutual love"... They'd have looked sorry, sympathetic...

But you must admit that we were prudence itself... we merely asked them... "What signs do you see of it? What makes you think it?"

And you got the expected answer: "Oh... just an impression... Was it false? Wasn't it mutual love?"

And there you lost your nerve... you looked as if you were protesting...

Only looked, that's all, without a word...

Just as well, otherwise from one word to the next you might have lured us into giving them this: "It's true, actually, you're right, what we feel for each other really is mutual love..."

And how can we even foresee what you're capable of in your moments of surrender, of submission... you'd have brought us to the point of giving them as a bonus: "great"... "a great love"...

132

You know very well that that wasn't possible... Let's imagine us trying to get hold of those words, "a great love"...

"A great love"... we focus on it... what's it like? It's great, but great in relation to what?

In relation to average ones, small ones...

In short, it's immense... we try to grasp it... it's heavy, slippery, shapeless...

We have to put it down on us, make it fit...

It's easy for it to be put down on them. To make room for it everything underneath becomes flattened, smoothed out, solidified... no rough edges, no protu-berances... "a great love" sticks to everything, overlies everything...

But with us it would be driven out, deported... we'd hear your cries, your warnings, be careful, there's something there that's going to collide with it, chip it, crack it, it'll be damaged, destroyed...

Our turbulent, ever-changing waves can bear no name.

What we feel isn't written down anywhere...

It passes... with no one any the wiser...

What an effort to try to recapture it... it would have to be resuscitated...

Whereas all they have to do is consult their diaries, which are always up-to-date... at any time they can extract from them and show...

And sometimes what they show astonishes us... You remember "I was suffering"...

Or "I was crying"...

When we were carried away, choking, blinded, incapable of looking inside ourselves... we had the impression that we didn't exist... *he* didn't lose sight of himself, he was capable of discovering that what was happening inside him is called "suffering"...

He was able to recognize from the damp warmth, the tickling sensation on his cheeks, that he was shedding tears... he preserved that, and now he's exhibiting it: "I was crying"...

And the "I'm really enjoying myself" that he suddenly let fall among us when we were fooling around, carefree, oblivious...

Without our realizing it, he'd gone off outside for a moment, to bring back that "I'm really enjoying myself" and imprison within it things that were dispersing, escaping...

"I'm really enjoying myself"... he went and declared it, gave it a name, and now he can come back and settle down among us again in all security. Everything is in order.

Isn't he like the child who suddenly, in the middle of a game, leaves his playmates, runs up to his mother, gets a kiss from her and goes back reassured, fortified...

Now, while he's preparing to rejoin our games, he's delighted to see what it contains, the thing he's brought back... it's so much appreciated, approved... it's so good, so beneficent, and it belongs to him and he's so pleased... "I'm really enjoying myself..."

But even more astonishing than "I'm really enjoying myself" was the "I shall really have enjoyed myself" that she suddenly flung at us at a moment when we were indeed "beside ourselves," we were so caught up in what we were seeing or hearing that was so very funny...

Even the people around us seemed amazed... they wouldn't have been able to say why...

It's so difficult to say... it takes time to discover what it's made of, "I shall really have enjoyed myself"... where its strength comes from...

From "shall have," obviously. From that future coming and ensconcing itself in the heart of the present...

What other languages possess such a precise, delicate instrument?

"I shall really have enjoyed myself"... to know how to use it you have to possess exceptional gifts, rare skill...

At one stroke, what was going to be done has been done... It stretches out behind us, immovable, proffered, like a memory... in order to see it you must look back...

It was piping hot, bubbling over... and she picked it, froze it, canned it... "I shall really have enjoyed myself"... she's already licking her lips... how delightful it will be to treat herself to it one day...

While we are there, spending without counting the cost, squandering without a thought, real prodigals, she is thinking of the future and making a good investment... "I shall really have enjoyed myself..."

The present moment has no value other than the promise it contains... a child one is only interested in because one sees in him the adult he will become...

What was fragile, perishable, which would have decomposed, disappeared... she has found a way to safeguard it... She has embalmed it, she has exhibited it in a glass coffin, she contemplates it with a tender, nostalgic shake of the head... "I shall really have enjoyed myself..."

And this one, coming back to us, running up to us along the path, holding out her hand, with the thumb apart... she comes up on to the terrace... everyone stands up, goes towards her, examines the gash on her thumb from which blood is flowing...

While we disinfect it, bandage it, she looks angry, stamps her foot...

No, she doesn't stamp her foot, you read that in books...

At any rate she looks furious, indignant... "Who did that to you?" "No one. I did it. With the pruning shears..." "Oh, that happened to me too, only the other day, when I was pruning the roses..." And then she yells... and don't say she doesn't yell...

That's true, she yells... "But that I should do it to *myself!*" and she runs off.

At the door she turns round and shouts at us... "You can't understand. That's the sort of thing that shouldn't happen to me!"

It's words like those that make people say "What a world!"

They probably don't realize how right they are... Those words open out on to a whole world...

A world that is so unlike our own...

Nothing up till now had shown us that she belongs to it...

When she makes her appearance in front of us she disguises herself... She preserves her incognito.

It took that accident to make her "fly off the handle," to make her show us who she is over there, in her place.

She holds the highest rank there.

140

But why? For what reasons?

How can we know on what rules they base their discrimination, their selection...

There must be certain characteristics, certain gifts, that are only possessed by superior people...

One single act, which he thinks insignificant, enables them to recognize an inferior...

What a lot of acts of that sort we must have performed...

She, quite naturally, never does them.

She couldn't allow herself to, without losing caste...

How she must have smiled to herself when we were trying to reassure her... "But you know, that happened to me too, only the other day, when I was pruning the roses..."

Smiled? Such stupid obliviousness to what we are... that's what comes of making an inferior believe that one is like him... so much impertinence must have increased her exasperation even more...

Nevertheless, we could have foreseen all that... There were nevertheless some signs...

When we didn't know the right way to use the can-opener... when we couldn't manage to screw up the stopper...

Her look when she took it out of our hands... "Don't bother, give it to me, that isn't the way, let me"...

An indulgent, scornful look...

And we were surprised... how strangely futile of her, how childish... Well yes, we are rather clumsy... What does it matter?

Certainly not a great deal to us... But to her... But how right we were to believe that the great are to be pitied...

And how we understand her now... That clumsy movement when she was using the pruning shears... How indecent, what a comedown!... "That's the sort of thing that shouldn't happen to me!"

"And that I should do it to myself..."

How lovingly he looked at his hand that he had spread out in front of us on the table...

He was one of the first who came when we called them...

When we wanted to make someone with the power to love himself appear in front of us...

A power we lack, it was only recently that we realized it.

This one running up to us now, holding out her injured hand, is a rarer, more astonishing model...

What she yells to us, "That I should do it to myself!" what that contains...

We only have to go to the trouble of taking it...

No, what a lot of trouble we'd have to go to!

So long as it isn't trouble for nothing.

So long as it's worth the trouble.

It's so good to beat about the bush like this...

Under cover of these reliable old expressions...

But that's enough shilly-shallying...

"That I should do it to myself!" "I" has done it to "Myself"... The duplication is clearer than ever, now...

The person who loves himself splits himself in two... projects his double outside... places it at a certain distance from himself...

So that it can fulfill certain functions...

And this time, the double hasn't fulfilled its function...

But what function was it, exactly?

That of frontier guard... you remember how he was keeping watch, seeing them coming from a distance, the people who were getting ready to go beyond the limits...

And now this ever-vigilant guard, she looks for him in vain... where has he gone?

He's gone over to the other side, he's joined the vulgar...

He, her double, has gone to demean himself, to mingle with his inferiors who are clumsy, ill-bred, incapable of controlling their movements, of using their ten fingers properly...

Here they are, coming up with him, all similar to him, they go right up to her, cling to her, look innocently, stupidly at her injured hand, they want to reas-

144

sure her... "You know, that happened to us too, the other day, when we were pruning the roses..."

But the main function that we should have...

How was it we didn't see it right away?

It was too obvious... as it is in that game where you're looking for, but can't find, an object that is there in front of you, staring you in the face...

Her bodyguard, whose duty it was to keep watch over every little bit of that beloved body, to protect it against the slightest attack...

That bodyguard himself wounded her... She finds herself in a situation in which anyone who had any sense, without bothering about what his words contained, would have pointed out to her that "she had only herself to blame"...

Only herself to blame! But what more painful, more dangerous can be imagined for someone who loves himself?

"If it were me, this is what I'd do"... That's what we expected, it was bound to happen... For a moment he observes the person we are discussing in front of him, he shakes his head the way people do when they say "Ah, what a thing to see"... and right away he turns to himself... "If it were me..."

In that darkness, that entanglement where the other has wandered, in which he's getting lost, he very soon opens up a path for himself, the right path, the direct path... "If it were me, this is what I'd do... I'd go and see the manager and tell him..."

Some of us immediately become restless... You who beat a retreat at the slightest sign of danger, who run and huddle up in the corners...

We can already feel suspicious, hostile glances reaching us... "It's not possible, he can't do that... What would his colleagues think of him? He'd be thought an informer, a traitor..." "But I'd have told them first, I'd have warned them that I wasn't going to put up with their bullying, their aspersions any longer... That if they continued, I should feel obliged... And then, if I saw that they hadn't taken the slightest notice, I should go in their presence... I should demand to be received..."

The manager's tone... "Come in!" The weight of his gaze bearing down on the person who appears at the door, who steps forward... "Would you dare? But how would you be received?" "I should be very well received, believe me. Obviously, if you look as if you are defeated in advance... But if it were me, I guarantee that he would listen. I would tell him that a limit had been reached and that from then on, either the others behaved decently, or I should be forced to offer..." "But that's just it, how could you risk...? How could you be sure of finding another?..." "Ah, when you prefer to put up with... but personally, if I'm pushed to the limit, there's nothing I'm not prepared to... I'm prepared to face anything..." "But not everyone has your determination, your strength."

We try once more to show him the poor unfortunate fellow trapped, trammelled, blinded, floundering, searching, giving up, despairing... He stretches, straightens his head, his back, he cracks his fingers... "What do you expect me to say? One thing is certain, which is that if it were me..."

Do we have to remind ourselves of all the situations, all the occasions we offered him?

It looks as if there is something in him that constrains us... we absolutely have to exhibit to him... "Don't you find that distressing?..."

He considers it for a moment, and then returns to himself... "If it were me, this is what I'd do..."

Can it be possible that he sees himself completely from outside as if he were a flesh and blood character?

Perhaps not... He doesn't place himself at that distance... he must feel a light emanating from him... He feels a force flowing out of him and infallibly triggering an action that takes place according to the prescriptions of morality, equity, generosity, dignity, lucidity, prudence...

Codes of laws whose every article he knows by heart and can apply to every case...

All the objections we raise make him think of paper screens that he tears as he makes his way through them one after the other.

Yes, but if it were me, I wouldn't attach any importance to...

If it were me, in spite of that I'd find room for...

If it were me, I wouldn't hesitate to dismiss...

If it were me, I'd hand out...

If it were me, I'd keep...

If it were me, I'd be on my guard...

If it were me, I'd keep quiet...

If it were me, I'd admit...

If it were me... If it were me... If it were me...

But it can happen that that "If it were me..." doesn't come. He turns away, he doesn't want to look, he purses his lips as if in disgust...

Disgust is too strong... he pulls back, his gaze becomes vacant... He refuses to take part...

150

We'd foreseen it... What the devil has got into you... going and finding that and bringing it up in front of him!...

As if we didn't know which people he doesn't want to have anything to do with... He has always avoided dubious company...

We could have been quite sure he would never agree to see himself in that situation. No "If it were me" when the person we are showing him is someone with "a warped mind"... someone who "sees evil every-where"...

But we had taken our precautions... "There's no mistake about it, you know, he's a son who respects, who loves his father dearly... and his father feels the same about him... It isn't possible that his father could be jealous of him, as some might think, he doesn't believe that for a moment, it isn't that at all, only the thing is...

He raises his eyebrows, he shows astonishment... he consents to dart a glance, and we take advantage of it... "What he feels in his father... and this is what stops him talking to him as he always has about what is close to his heart, you understand... His father is the only person to whom he has always liked to tell... he even wants to boast about it a little... and now he can't let himself go any more... what he feels in his father... and this is what holds him back... is... is... something like nostalgia, melancholy... something like... not suffering, no, that's too strong... it's something humble, something defenseless... well, he doesn't know what it is but he doesn't want to see it... And so he avoids telling him... or else he deliberately belittles himself, he covers up... with his father... he's afraid of arousing... He feels compelled to keep at a certain distance... it's a rift that hurts him... It creates a gulf between his father and him... Perhaps it would be better to ignore it... Perhaps if he were to talk to him as if nothing had happened, he might manage to...

But it's from a great distance that he's watching you writhing in front of him. You're so over-eager that you finally make him confuse us with the other. He feels we're indistinguishable... And as always, we are obliged to "save face"... We make you come back and lose no time in presenting him with a serene look, an indulgent smile, only a trifle haughty... We give a sigh... "And anyway, I wonder why he mentioned it to me... That sort of relationship is so different from the ones I have with my family, especially with my father... he's always so proud of his children's slightest success... the best, the most normal of fathers... I didn't know what to answer... I wondered whether you..."

Then he flung out his arms and said: "Oh, me you know, such things... they're beyond me..."

The things he leaves outside, they shouldn't be allowed to enter... things you can't make out very well... you don't know what they are, what to call them...

They're all soft, squashy, mushy, when you set foot on them you get sucked down... swamps...

Caustic soda in which you're going to dissolve...

A swarm of evasive things that hide in dark holes, dank crevices...

And there's nothing in him into which they can insinuate themselves... everything in him is clean, clear, well lit, tidy, catalogued.

His familiar interior world, which from time to time he can amuse himself with by inventorying...

Where he likes to be...

It's only after we have observed how much mistrust, repulsion, there is towards these things, that we have been able to imagine how they are seen by people who say that they are "beyond" them...

They aren't "beyond" *us*. They are in us... our substance...

When we manage to catch sight of them for a moment as they would appear to us if we could observe ourselves, they don't make us think of frightening swarms, of furtive evasions...

They are impervious to words like furtive, frightening, repugnant...

Such things might make you think of the multitude of tiny stitches on an ever-moving canvas that will go on being woven for ever... will always stretch farther and farther...

Nothing there that's either impure or pure... either good or evil. These things cannot be qualified. No adjective can be applied to them, nor any name.

They come from no matter where... nothing can stop them... no partition... they can't in any way be filtered... No one is there to see this arrive, to make it stay...

They always find a familiar environment in us, where close friends, relations live...

But with him, you have to be checked before you're allowed in...

However hard you try... No no, you can let him in, it isn't what you think, not at all, it wasn't jealousy he sensed in his father, nothing so unhealthy, so unpleasant... we know very well that you don't allow admission to that sort of thing... no, it's rather what might be called...

And you presented it to him wrapped up in mumbles, in mutters... it's... it's melancholy, nostalgia...

Still that illusion that somewhere inside him there must be reception centers where such things, however slight, however modest, unobtrusive, could be entertained without danger...

Whereas they are precisely the ones that seem to him the most dangerous... And when you plucked up the courage to add that what he perceives in his father is something defenseless, something humble...

He grasped it at once, no point in hiding it from him... what this son sees in his father arouses in him what is called "pity." That's its real name... His father arouses pity in him. A feeling it is shocking to have for one's father...

Do you think it was "pity" that he found?

But of course, he didn't have to search for it for very long in his registers...

He knows where it comes from... from those regions of ill repute...

Peopled by God knows whom, outlaws, pariahs...

And that's where they're trying to drag him... among those shameless people who dare to raise their eyes to their denuded father...

People who lack the respect owed to a father, the respect owed to oneself...

And we... How can we know whether we are lacking in respect... Here, nothing has a name. No one has any function. Here there is neither father nor mother.

Only the feeling that something in us is tending, extending, is going to enter the auspicious regions where it will grow, blossom...

But in the place it has entered the air is heavy, confined, it's dark... and everything is becoming atrophied, wizened, shrivelled, twisted...

What would there be for them to do here, where would they find their place, the words: Father. Pity. Respect...

Still those same emaciated arms being held out, those washed-out eyes from which tears are coursing, that trembling voice... "Take me with you..."

At other times it's sobs, entreaties, a child's arms held out towards us...

Or again...

But what's the good of recalling everything that comes back to us at times and revives the same stabbing pain in us...

Agonizing twinges like the ones that suddenly return in a certain point in our body...

We prod, we press... it hurts...

But not like we are hurt... not in the same way as we are hurt by all the apparitions of entreating arms and faces bathed in tears that come to us from all over the world.

It's something we ourselves have created...

We have manufactured it... And we have wounded ourselves with it... It's made a deep gash in us...

Splinters have entered us and become embedded, there's no way to extract them.

And yet, when it was still incomplete, we could have transformed it, we were going to do so, we were going to lean over and let those emaciated old arms raised up to us hug our shoulders, let the child's arms be clasped around our neck... let smiles and words radiate appeasement, tenderness...

But you intervened... You poured lead into those arms that were going to throw themselves around us... We could already feel how we were sagging under their embrace, we were staggering, were going to fall, remain prostrate, unable to get up...

And we allowed them to become what they remained for ever... those helpless arms stretched out towards us, those heartrending appeals...

We have turned them into that petrified thing. Immutable.

No fluctuations. Never anything nebulous, cloudy, nothing obscure, no shadow...

A hard object. Very distinct. Sharp.

Made of an unalloyed material, which bears a name everyone knows: "Abandon."

It entered into us and has become part of us... a point in us where at times an incurable pain returns...

But the person who loves himself... how is it possible not to envy him when he describes to us those arms stretched out towards him, those eyes full of tears which sometimes appear to him too... "Yes, I feel remorseful... it makes me feel remorseful, the way I behaved, what I did... or didn't do, rather... I didn't have my sick mother to live with me... I refused to look after my child... I was selfish. I was a coward." And he shakes his head with an air of reproval... of repulsion, even...

Does he disgust himself? Does he hate himself?

We know very well that he can have such moments... But what does that change? He still brings everything back to himself, it's himself he's looking at...

What he sees there makes him look ugly... he doesn't like it...

It makes him angry... And it may even happen...

We've noticed that more than once... it may happen that he also gets angry with the people who were responsible for this unpleasant feeling in him... who are the cause of his remorse... they irritate him... He resents them for having made him become the way he now sees himself...

If they hadn't pushed him, he wouldn't have made that stain...

It's them, rather than himself, that he seems to love less because they showed him their entreating arms, because they made him hear their appeals...

As for him, if he hates himself, it's in the same way as we sometimes hate the people we love... whom we can't stop loving...

160

We love them just as they are... Ah, what can I do, I am what I am...

Sometimes, when he's showing us the way he is, he looks like those people who are privileged to own a gallery of portraits of their ancestors and who enjoy showing them... Look, that one, he was a real brigand who feared neither God nor man... He didn't stop at anything, he abandoned his wife and children... And that one, she was a real saint... "Well yes, there are some sides to me... I can be hard. Cruel. I'm overcome by remorse every time I think about it... She was a loving mother and I loved her. I was ungrateful. I was selfish."

Is it possible to imagine one of us spouting to the outside world... "Yes, it's true, that wasn't good..." and getting us to nod our agreement... "Yes, you're right, you shouldn't have done that..."

Then how he flinches, what a haughty air, what a look... What business is it of yours? Like the parent whose child has behaved badly and who intimates to strangers that they shouldn't intervene, he is the only one who can deal with it... and he deals with it ruthlessly...

You can see how severely—spare the rod and spoil the child—he punishes himself...

A lucid, perfectly righteous judge who doesn't hesitate to punish what he holds most dear in all the world...

He's also someone who knows how to keep his house in order... "I know myself..." Then sometimes, before casting the first stone... "Who is perfect?"

And what a relief for the criminal when he kneels in the middle of the marketplace and allows his crime, his misfortune to escape from him and spread over the crowd that receives it, takes part in it.

But might one not think that in his gaze, still focused on himself, there appears something like tenderness, nostalgia?... "Ah yes, no doubt about it, I behaved badly... every time I think about it... I was young, very hare-brained..." he sees himself walking rapidly towards the door, almost running in the corridor, tearing down the stairs, breathing in the exciting outside air, dashing off, getting into trains, cars, on to liners... the whistling of the engines, the humming of the planes is exhilarating... it's the call of life... of his life... While down there, ever farther away, the entreating arms, the faces bathed in tears, dwindle, become blurred...

It was so unexpected, coming from him...

From him, when he might have been one of those people who get us to contemplate their hand spread out on the table...

One of those who when they are still children paint their self-portrait...

Of those who never allow anything to enter or leave their premises without subjecting it to meticulous inspection...

Who have always kept us outside the circle they have drawn around themselves, which we have never tried to cross... or even dreamed of crossing...

He whom we only ever saw from the distance from which he must see himself: solidly built. Stable. Well balanced. Sure of himself. Satisfied... why wouldn't he be?... to be what he is.

And suddenly he comes up very close to us, he leans over towards us, he looks deep into our eyes and allows these words to escape him, words trembling with anxiety, with distress... "Do you too... Do you know what it is? There are people... have you known any? I believe they're what's called slippery... When you're unlucky enough to come across one of them... when you become fond of him... you're lost..."

Something must have happened to him... have been produced in him... a fire, a conflagration... for him to dash up to us like that so carelessly dressed... "lost, do you hear me? lost"...

Lost... the word reverberates all through us... we rush up from all sides, we come together... someone there is appealing for help, someone is wanting to take refuge with us, he's calling... "Do you know that? Suddenly, when you least expect it... no matter when... in the course of a conversation... when you're relaxed, confident, letting yourself go... and all of a sudden you feel that something in the other is beginning to stir... he wants to stand aside, he's going to leave, to withdraw... What are you thinking about? we hang on, we can't let him go... Do you see?"

We search inside ourselves... where is it? Where is the place in which that can be welcomed, given treatment...

We make haste, we shall find it... what can't we find here? there's really something of everything...

It's been overlooked somewhere, it's a long time since we went over on that side, we must look carefully...

It must be here... A disused place, uninhabited for so many years...

He's still calling, he's suffering... "Every time it's a breach, you understand, a break..."

Ah, here it is... we've found it... we nod our assent... "It's like a crevice opening up... however hard you try you can't get over it, its edges move apart, it's widening..."

He leans even farther forward, he whispers in our ear... "You know, I'm going to tell you... it seems crazy, but it would be less painful if one knew where the other was going... even if it was to meet someone... but when it's just to escape... do you see? just to get away no one knows where... to be away from you..."

That we can't see very well... where was it? where's it gone? Then suddenly we catch sight of it... we find it... we feel that the other is going to lose himself in nothingness... A vacuum... A vacuum that our absence fills... where we are abolished... we no longer exist... "Yes, you're right... what the other is seeking is our disappearance..." "That's it, you've seen it... And then, when one has reached that point, when one is in that state, what can one do?"

It's a long time since we have had anything to do with such a case... A serious case... how did we treat it? we can only see old remedies... Had they been any use? Had they cured...?

We hesitate as we offer them... "You can try... it's unpleasant to swallow... you have to start with very small doses... to take the initiative in bringing about short separations, look forward to them even, make the first move... you'll see what a relief it is, there can be no more breaks... you start living on terra firma again. No threats possible now, no fears... Such security, such serenity..."

He seems annoyed, he shakes his head in exasperation... "Ah, so that's what you're suggesting? I've already tried it, it wasn't any good... I acted as if I were distancing myself of my own free will, taking the first steps myself... and it didn't work... I didn't feel relieved and it didn't bring the other back, it didn't frighten him..." "But that wasn't what we were advising you, it wasn't that at all, that's a quack remedy... the other immediately sees what you're up to, he detects the subterfuge, he knows you too well... You needed to detach yourself for good, and especially to give up all desire, not expect him to come back... Even if only for a short time, to manage to feel free, happy..." "Happy! Without him! That's impossible... You know very well that 'one person's lost to you, and no one else exists'... I can't..." "Ah, it's difficult, it demands a great effort, a lot of strength..."

These words, coming from us... we ourselves are surprised by them... seem to give him a shock... he wakes up, he comes to... Where was he? How far had he allowed himself to go? And to whom? Whom had he been to to ask for a remedy? Whom had he allowed into his premises? To search... to get hold of what? And then to go off and exhibit it, so proud of possessing such a treasure, an original piece, unique, impossible to find. He throws himself back, he settles back comfortably in his armchair, he observes us, there's suspicion, almost hostility in his look... "I don't know why I had to talk to you about that... to exaggerate... I gave importance to something that has none... these moments of 'passion'..." he pronounces the word ironically... "these little crises are soon over..." He seems to be turning back to himself and examining himself... "To tell the truth, on the whole my temperament is that of a hunter... or of a gun-dog... anything that runs away excites me, I want to catch it... And then, once I've got it... and even when I haven't got it... Well, it doesn't take long..." He makes the gesture with his hand that denotes rejection, insouciance.

And yet we were on safe ground... extremely well-trodden ground...

Where we had done nothing that wasn't permissible, normal, and even well thought of.

It's impulses like that one that must make people say that we are someone nice, generous.

But it wasn't even generous, it was quite simply decent... Why keep to ourselves, why not show him our gratitude for the pleasure he gave us... "a delight..."

Delight... was that actually the word that was used? it's hard to remember...

Yes yes, it actually was delight. "A delight to see so much courage, independence..."

That could only have been said in a tone vibrant with sincerity... a tone that ought to have made him feel that what we said "came from the heart"...

Then all of a sudden that movement he made as if to protect himself... that cutting, glacial "Thank you very much" that he pressed on us...

His look, which quickly rounded us up and compressed us into one... and then he eyed this "one" with scorn... What's that? Who is this individual who has dared to trespass... uninvited...

He's one of those who had no other right than to judge from his own seat and to let the people around him know his emotions...

But he thought he was entitled to come up close to me, to touch me... a contact which brought a flush to my cheeks, impossible to prevent it...He noticed it... He thought he had immediately found the sensitive chord in me and he made it vibrate... "It's true, it's no exaggeration to say that it was a delight... So much courage, independence..."

We had had the audacity to inspect him and to take in our hands, to appraise like connoisseurs... "you own some superb pieces there, you're to be congratulated..."

And how could he be certain that we hadn't said the same thing to someone else, to God knows whom... Someone, however praiseworthy he might be, has been placed by us in the same rank, put on the same footing as him. Him, the unique. The incomparable.

But what if, in spite of the perfect sincerity of our tone, we had been trying to gull him... What if he had been duped... if we had been delighted to see him swallowing what we gave him, stretching out greedily...

Isn't there something astonishing about the fact that we had no presentiment, not the slightest apprehension...

That we were so flabbergasted to have been thanked in that way...

That it could happen to *us,* not to have recognized... not to have foreseen...

To throw ourselves like fools, like innocents, at someone who loves himself...

Who really loves himself?

Of course he loves himself, he's demonstrated it...

But in such a painful, uneasy way, which obliges himself to protect himself so carefully, to be permanently on his guard.

A self-love so supercilious, so suspicious, that it didn't allow him to accept in all simplicity, with pleasure, our sincere, spontaneous praise.

Shouldn't it be thought that in this art of loving oneself, he has only what might be called talent? A minor talent, no more...

If we compare him with one of those people who we can say without exaggeration loves himself with genius...

So close to perfection that he ought to serve us as a model, if only we were capable of trying to love ourselves...

Let's watch him receiving our compliments...

He doesn't examine us to see who we are. Whether we are worthy of getting really close to him, of touching him.

172

Does a sovereign refuse to let his hand be shaken by any other hand held out to him when he's responding to the adoration of the crowd?

He ought rather to be moved by our obscurity, by the modesty of our situation.

And by the sincerity of our tone.

Oh, so far as sincerity is concerned, wouldn't he think that goes without saying?

If we had offered him our compliments in a stiff, awkward manner, that oughtn't to have displeased him...

He would simply have seen that we are intimidated, that we are impressed...

That we still haven't enough practice, that we still haven't acquired the assurance, the good manners in his presence of the people he usually frequents...

But even if he doubted our sincerity, he wouldn't take the trouble to bother with us, to delve into us, to probe, like the person who only loves himself with talent, to make sure that we aren't trying to gull him...

How could he imagine us observing him while he's swallowing our praises?

173

See himself becoming pink with satisfaction...
stretching out greedily...

For the person who loves himself with genius, the
flattering words we address to him are a gage, a guarantee, the sign of our submission, of our adhesion... they
are our oath of allegiance...

He receives our compliments as offerings we have
come to lay at his feet, he looks at them, and he inclines
his head with an air of approval, of benevolence, he
thanks us and then turns, and passes on to the next
one...

What she has is genius... Not merely talent, talent wouldn't be enough... she loves herself with genius, which is where that comes from...

We had never suspected it before. None of the people around her can ever have suspected it, no one would dare think it...

It's her love of herself, so absolute, so powerful, that radiates from her and is communicated to everyone around her... That's what produces in everyone without exception that confidence in her, that love for her, that unqualified admiration...

We feel so excited, we feel we'd like to skip, to cheer, it's an illumination, a revelation...

The most unexpected...

It's still confused, dispersed... we don't know how to get hold of it, where to grasp it...

By her look... that look when she turns it on to herself... And what she sees gives her that barely perceptible smile, she smiles at herself, she nods her head gently... with a tender, slightly surprised air... By what grace of Heaven has she been made thus? How can one be so very...

So very what?

She doesn't try to find words to describe it... She doesn't need them...

She doesn't particularly want to show it to us... She really forgets we're there, she's entirely concentrated on what she sees...

And what she sees, what is there under her gaze, is something obvious. Unquestionable.

Something adorable... of touching, astonishing perfection...

176

Then all of a sudden, her pout of disgust...

It looks as if she's shivering inside herself, shrinking, drawing aside... but from what? What on earth can there be, in what we brought her... simply to divert her, to amuse her... it seemed so harmless...

Yes, to us... But she saw in it... there's something there... what can it possibly be? something ugly, repugnant... "You don't like it, do you? You think people ought not to behave in that way? You think it wasn't good, what he did?"

She turns back to herself... she takes her time...

She wants to make sure of what is indicated to her by that perfect instrument of impeccable precision... that infallible way of testing with which she has been endowed by a generous fate and which enables her without the slightest possible risk of error to distinguish between good and evil.

She listens to the decree pronounced by the law court that is in permanent session inside her and which in every case that comes before it administers laws that are the laws of Heaven.

She shakes her head... that's the way it is, she can't help it, she can only communicate its conclusions to us... inform us of its sentence... "No. It wasn't good."

These words produce in us what certain sacred texts produce in believers... they're surprised, disconcerted, but they soon give in, it's beyond them, who are we to take the liberty of...? they cross themselves piously, how could we have dared? may we be forgiven...

We bow, we accept, there's no question of us casting doubt on it.

We would just like to see it too, we hadn't noticed it, it had escaped us... if only she would be good enough to show it to us, what she'd seen, what she'd disliked...

But we know we won't get anything...

Nothing other than what we have already received... in her look turned in towards what she sees in herself, there will once again be that expression of remoteness, of repulsion... she'll shake her head, she'll say: "Oh, I don't know..."

Obviously, "these are things that can't be explained," "you either feel it or you don't." And our questions will only increase, they will only add weight to, plant more deeply in her, what she has already probably grasped in us and taken away...

178

It may perhaps remain in her...

It will turn her away from us, our crudeness, our atrophied sensitivity, our indifference to the contact of what is evil, what is ugly...

How is it that she has never yet rejected us, kept us at a distance?

We must have... but in what way? how? compensated... atoned...

Why does she still allow us to be amongst the people she has chosen to keep with her?

The elect... very few...

Whom she has chosen and brought together... Yet we seem so dissimilar...

But the elect have something in common: an identical belief.

They are all absolutely certain that she knows... she cannot be wrong... no one can know better than she... she knows what's good, what's evil.

But now that it has suddenly descended into us... that illumination... everything has immediately become clear...

And what we have seen will never be effaced.

It wasn't only from her look, from her way of informing us of the sentence...

We were clinging on to the most salient thing that we could single out...

What emanates from her everywhere is diffused by her whole being.

Radiations... we were all irradiated...

Her love for herself had contaminated us...

Can we ever know how these sorts of contagion occur?

How cures are produced?

We can say that we owe ours to a miracle... can we give any other name to what happened to us, to that sudden revelation?

The others who were affected as we were—it doesn't seem possible to save them.

Does anyone remember anybody, trapped as we were, who was liberated?

Anybody who didn't always keep buried within himself, without really knowing what it was, that same muted, diffused anxiety...

That at any moment, without it ever being possible for him to discover for what shortcoming, for what sin, it might happen that he would be banished...

Dismissed by her into outer darkness.

Through those words applied to him... through the effect those words produced, that was how for the first time we saw...

Glimpsed, rather... we were flabbergasted... we still didn't have enough experience.

The man who pronounced those words... but what's the good of making the effort to describe him? It was one of the ones sitting with us, who must have been observing him for a while—he was sitting at another table—who suddenly said to us: "When you get a chance, watch him, he's over there talking to some friends... In my opinion there's something false, evasive... I'd even say something sly... in his eyes, in the movement of his lips..."

Ordinary words pronounced in a tone of impartial observation, certainly in all innocence...

In all thoughtlessness... He, like us, must have been surprised when they laughed so very loudly... "How amusing, you're priceless... To hear someone talking like that about him... to say that he isn't straightforward! that he's sly! if we were to tell that..." Then he asked them: "Why? Do you think he's very sincere? very straightforward?"

They laughed even more loudly... "This gets funnier and funnier... oh come on, you've got it all wrong, completely wrong... sly, false, sincere, straightforward, none of such notions can apply to him, you must forget them... but how can you not feel it? Don't you realize that he can't be qualified, he can't be judged like just anyone... He's out of the common run, he's above, beyond... He's an exceptional being... People have called him... and it's no exaggeration... a 'supernatural' man... and you didn't know it?"

And then when we were taken to his house, on our way there, what happened...

184

Or rather what didn't happen... the lack of all pre-caution, of all preparation...

As if we were going to visit just anyone.

No warning... don't talk about this or that in front of him, don't bring up that subject, don't touch it, and don't say that you like a certain person when he doesn't like him, or that you don't like him, when he does like him...

Words of courtiers, of servants, for whom the thoughts, the feelings of their master are merely his particularities, his prejudices, his caprices, his whims, his idiosyncrasies... It's useful, it's necessary to know them, to take them into consideration, but there's nothing there that can penetrate deeply enough into them... can arouse a feeling, a thought in them that would be prepared to confront... to oppose...

That would force a word out of them, make a silence seep out of them and spread around them in which the master would detect a certain reticence... Just a hint of resistance...

Nothing that could cause him the slightest irritation...

But the people they have had the audacity to choose to introduce to him must be warned... be careful, be on the alert at all times, don't forget that at every moment you make us run a terrible risk...

At best, a certain loss of confidence. A reprimand... "How could you have brought him to my place? Where can you have got that ridiculous idea..."

At worst, a lasting grudge, an insuperable cooling-off.

But this time, none of all that. No trace of the attitude of a courtier. No precautions. Just as if we were being taken to see a friend with whom it was reasonable to expect it would be possible for us to have "fruitful exchanges."

But when we went into his place...

There was no way we could have realized it at the time...

Going into his place, we got a stage further.

We advanced into the interior of this unknown region we had entered, quite bowled over, just for a moment, that day, when suddenly from all around we heard people laughing at very ordinary words... "sly," "evasive"... that a thoughtless fellow had flung at him...

Bursts of laughter had intercepted those words, had deflected them before they'd been able to reach him...

And in the place of those words, enormous, imposing words were introduced... "An exceptional man," "A supernatural man" to erect an impassable rampart around him. And give him permanent protection.

From the moment we came face to face with him...

It doesn't seem as if that ever happened to us...

By his mere presence...

Without our being able to detect the slightest movement in him...

Without him seeming to be aware...

By his mere existence, there, in front of us, he dispossessed us... He completely invaded us, occupied us...

Nothing, anywhere, belongs to us any longer. Everything belongs to him. He is the absolute master, everywhere he does whatever he likes...

Moving around wherever the whim takes him... Stopping here or there... looking... What's that?

It came to him all of a sudden, no one knows how... or perhaps one of the people there with us decided it would be a good idea to summon into his presence and submit to him...

In any case, the moment it had been called by its name...

The moment it is pronounced, that name makes us see snatches, vestiges of what had belonged to us when we were at home... A little humpback bridge above greenish water... the golden curves of a cupola... a fountain in a little square paved with big, silky flagstones...

Well, almost any of the many things that used to belong to us... so many places we have preserved in which we can take refuge at any moment...

It comes back in an instant... For an instant it remains there...

He's looking... is that what he's seeing?

He slightly raises his hand...

A single one of his gestures... a shrug of the shoulders, a pout, every one of his words, everything that comes from him has such power...

He raises his hand, he lowers it and says: "I've never understood some people's craze for..."

188

What comes out of these words sweeps away, obliterates at one stroke... everything has disappeared... and in the empty space in front of us a town is built under his orders... *His* town... And it's our town too, now.

But we haven't the slightest desire to wander around in it, he mustn't think that, we are not part of those sheeplike crowds who file over the little old bridges, lean over the greenish water, raise their heads to contemplate the curves of the cupolas outlined against the blue sky, smack their lips in appreciation when they run their hands over the rounded edges of the fountains, darkened, made greasy by so many touches...

We too see how everything over there is covered with a thin coating, a film...

Made up of all those contacts, descriptions, and reproductions.

There is something in what appears through it... What can it be?

All we can manage to say is that when we look at it we feel... disappointment... a lack...

A slight repugnance...

Almost a sort of degradation...

Degradation?

No, that isn't too strong a word. In what is being displayed before us under its delicate, shiny coating, there is something degrading.

Fortunately he doesn't linger, he's already some way away, and we with him, we stop like he does, we look...

That was also part of our possessions... Faraway possessions which we crossed rapidly, delighted not to have to stay there, in those expanses of greyness, rockiness, bushiness as far as the eye can see... not to have to live in one of those isolated houses, a cement cube without a garden... "All this space is mine... I found this house one day when I was out for a walk, some twenty years ago, I'm sorry not to be able to spend more time here, I have a soft spot for these regions..."

And we immediately... even the least flexible, the most sluggish of us, we tear ourselves away...

We don't tear ourselves away, the force in him lifts us up, we are thrown out of our homeland...

Deprived of the gentle pleasures we used to bask in, soothed by the rustling of leaves, of young branches,

190

caressing petals, breathing in the scent of roses... Accumulating all the objects, furniture, knick-knacks which we held dear... which we held on to...

We were attached to them, bound to them, they were a part of ourselves...

A precious part...

Perpetually menaced... We had to keep a constant watch on it, keep it under surveillance... The thing that had always been there has disappeared, perhaps it's been moved, no, it's been removed, it's been annihilated, and there, there's a vacuum in its place now, but here, it's cracked, it's fissured, torn...

And we are cracked, fissured, torn...

In an instant we have left all that, and how much more than that—we could go on describing it for ever—we have left it behind us...

We've been dragged out of it, not proud of having lived in it, rather ashamed of having been so softened, submissive, scared.

Here, where he's transported us, our gaze can rove over these immense empty plains, wander absentmindedly over these bare walls, slide along these straight lines...

Lines that flow, that fly... they don't slow down to bend, to incurve over us, to protect us under their calm, reassuring curves...

No fascinating objects that attract us, cling to us...

Become dear to our hearts... speak to our hearts...

But what words! they've escaped from the place where we were so snug...

Words which seem imbued with insipid, sickly-sweet scents...

Like suspect traces, trails of dubious nostalgic feelings...

But it was nothing, only a few whiffs rising from the old rancid refuse remaining in our nooks and crannies, they've been swept away, we've been cleansed, completely filled with one single pure nostalgia, that of living by his side, wherever he wishes to live...

Where nothing dares to touch him, to ask anything of him, to speak to him... Nothing can threaten his independence... Restrict his freedom.

It's that life that is "real" life. The only one it is permissible to call "worth living." The life lived by the strong, the pure, such as him.

192

But who can have so much purity, strength?

He is planted in front of us, very straight. Stable. Immutable.

In the vacuum around him he takes on enormous dimensions.

You might think he was made of one single substance, it has such unity, such cohesion. An enormous block, all in one piece.

Nothing can be detached from it to be examined, described...

Developing in him...

He secretes them... thoughts made to his measure, great thoughts that fly high, get lost in the distance...

Too far in the distance sometimes for us to be able to follow them...

He's still amusing himself by striding with his giant's steps over the entire world. He travels through time in all directions...

And we run after him, we try hard not to let him get too far ahead of us, we hurry to catch him up... we watch in amazement as with a disdainful kick he makes them wobble, collapse... things we had always seen as indestructible... had anyone ever dreamed of attacking them?

We watch them topple... we shall have to bury them... whole epochs, civilizations.

Others, that have long been lying buried, neglected, he sees fit to revive, they stand up obediently, they appear before him, he contemplates them, he nods... what merit they had, what charm... and we too contemplate them, we approve, respectful, fascinated...

We don't flinch... only occasionally a quickly-suppressed gasp... we abandon to their fate venerated personalities suddenly cast out by him, banished.

We're ready, we're getting there, we shall be capable of recognizing, honoring those people who up to now have been obscure, stupidly despised, whom he has chosen to summon to take the front seats...

We, and everyone making a circle with us around him.

All of us silent, eclipsed...

Snared by him, completely absent from themselves...

194

Hypnotized by him, performing all his movements...

He's stopped speaking, he seems a little weary, he's tired, even he, so resistant...

We do hope he isn't getting bored... what could we entertain him with?

Someone beside us has found... at least he seems to think he has... in any case he's dared to take the risk... he's gone to fetch, not very far away, no need to tire oneself by travelling great distances any more... the person he brings us is quite close, we're all familiar with him, he's one of our old acquaintances...

The moment his name is pronounced, he appears...

Like everyone whom we summon up, whom we summon to our presence, he can appear under so many different aspects...

This time, what we see is the rapid sketch of a tall, slim figure in a dark, rather loose overcoat... his barely-visible features express what might be called dignity, perhaps hauteur... the narrow slits between his drooping eyelids reveal benevolence, even goodness...

But why him? Why weren't we afraid that this insignificant, banal character would create... would produce even more boredom? Where did it come from, that confident tone of voice in which he was introduced... "I believe you've known him for a long time... When he heard I was going to meet you, he told me about the years you spent together some time ago, when he was your colleague... how important they had been to him... everything you did for him... Every time he meets you again he feels the same..."

Does he already know, while he is pronouncing these words, what is going to happen?

No! Impossible. It can never have happened before. It would have been known. We should have heard of it.

That confidence can only have been the result of one of those incomprehensible, supernatural premonitions...

Certainly unconscious... he doesn't know, he can't know why it came to him... a sudden inspiration...

In any case, the result is immediate... That gaze which we were so upset to see fading, becoming aloof, returns rekindled, brilliant, alights, becomes fixed... "Of course I've known him for years... an old chum... He used to lend me his room when he was away, when

196

he went on holiday... I used to go there to be alone, to work in peace... And do you know..." He has completely revived, he's even excited, he leans over towards us... "It's extremely curious... Do you know, one day I took it into my head to light a fire in his stove... There was a big parcel in it, wrapped up in thick brown paper... I took it out, it was his private diary... very private, even, in which he'd written the things no one ever admits to... he described himself in situations... of the most humiliating kind possible... He was reaching, as he said, the extreme point of humiliation..."

Images appear, very old images come up from a common stock... they hover suspended...

Probably not quite the same in front of each of the people around us... different sketches that each of them has made from a single model enclosed within us all for a long time...

They brush up against us, here and there they give rise to the irrepressible little laughs that come from being tickled... children's excited giggles...

He shakes his head gently, indulgently... "But you know, you mustn't think... there's nothing of a Baron de Charlus about him, he doesn't direct the operations himself... these humiliations are not inflicted on him by his orders... He really suffers from them. He has been beaten, slapped... he could have hit back but he didn't hit back... He says that it wasn't out of fear... and he has come to believe that he provokes them unwittingly... he re-examines every case... I must say that there are some pretty comic ones..." He laughs, and this time we don't hold our laughter back... "The thing is that he always looks so dignified, so proud, even rather haughty, inclined to be scornful... And so to imagine him..." "Well yes, I must admit it's rather funny... Unexpected... But it shouldn't be such a great surprise... Everyone knows that a haughty attitude is sometimes a compensation... It counterbalances... Novelists have seen that, they've shown it. Obviously, in life we are obliged to rely on appearances. How can we know? For me, it took that combination of circumstances... one of those strokes of luck that lead to discoveries..."

There are smiles all round when we leave him...

An air of amusement, of satisfaction, of complicity is still playing over our faces when we part, outside...

Taking with us what he has had the generosity to give us, the present he gave us all...

The secret he did us the honor of entrusting to us...

A secret? But he never for a moment suggested that we should keep it...

198

And yet it's very likely that we shall all keep it.

They wouldn't be able to escape from the world made to their measure which they've returned to, in which they have always lived a circumscribed life, they'll never dare break its rules...

Especially those concerning respect for other human beings, which for them, "human brothers," is the same as self-respect.

They'd be recaptured, given a severe sentence...

It would be no use their trying to justify themselves by pleading that their only crime was to want to share what they'd received from him... they have it from his hand, and what a hand!

The only result of their mentioning his name would be to bring the barest suspicion of a smile to the lips, the eyes, of their judges... who would be watching them trying miserably to boast of, to pride themselves on being among the privileged number permitted to get close to him, to pick up what he throws them... for whatever reasons, according to whatever whim...

And if... but what an effort it takes to imagine it, it's so incredible, so unbelievable... if, carried away even further by the fear of being convicted, they went so far as to try to divert all the attention away from themselves, to focus it on him alone... Let's just try for a moment to look at him under the guise he took on, that of an equal, that of a fellow-creature, when he appeared in the room a friend had lent him, bending down to open the door of the stove, noticing, pulling towards him, taking out the mysterious parcel, well wrapped up and tied with string, taking the thick exercise book out of it, avidly turning its pages over, reading, more and more excited...

Doesn't it apply to him as it does to everybody else... doesn't it get irresistibly attracted and stick to him... what can only be called Indiscretion, Indelicacy?

But all they can manage to see, raising their heads very high, are minute scraps, little bits of paper on which must be written... we can't see them very well, they're too far away... the words Indelicacy, Indiscretion, which don't touch the immense body of the giant, but flutter, fall again...

If, becoming more and more agitated, discarding all prudence, they tried, the miserable dwarfs, to pick up and throw at him something even bigger, even heavier, Ignoble Ingratitude. Repugnant Denunciation. Cynicism. Sadism... it wouldn't make any impact on him. It would fall back on them, cover them...

They would be picked up again, in a dreadful state, and this time convicted of attempted profanation, sacrilege.

But what's the good of trying to imagine such attacks...

Which it wouldn't occur to anyone to carry out.

What might well happen, though, is that one of the people to whom he appeared would like to see him again, to watch him again with some of the others who were there, who had witnessed that astonishing apparition...

They would all see him again, then, leaning over them from his immense height, bending down, seizing at his feet and holding up in the air between two fingers a little manikin of the same size as the rest of them, stripped of his clothes, his bare flesh shivering and turning red while he rolls him over from one side to the other, observing him... "It's interesting, the contrast between the aspect we usually see of him, his air of haughty elegance, of perfect dignity... it's a compensation, it counterbalances the humiliations... one of those curious, amusing contradictions..."

The little manikin himself, if, against all possibility, it were to come to his ears that he had been the object of this demonstration, that he had been seized in that way, held up in the air, exhibited, we can, we must be certain that it would have no effect on him... just as if he hadn't heard anything, as if nothing had taken place, nothing that could have been remembered, reported on...

Nothing had been introduced into him that could have caused him to feel hostility, vindictiveness, that could have incited him, as if he were the equal of the big man, to rise up against him, that could make him lose his sense of proportion to the point of going and trying his strength against him, confronting him, attacking him...

No resentment, either, which would have made him depart, withdraw, exclude himself of his own free will, punish himself... who else?... and go and mull it all over, sulk by himself in his corner.

Perhaps, in that motionless, compact, homogeneous, very pure mass which completely fills him, which nothing has been able to shake, to fissure, however little, to chip... perhaps if we look sufficiently intensely we might perceive... no, though, it isn't an illusion, it really is there... something is just barely moving, just a slight quiver... as if of contentment, of pride...

Of gratitude towards that man, who is so great, who rediscovered him, insignificant as he is, when he thought himself forgotten, thrown on the scrap heap...

and yet he was always there somewhere, he was a part of those mysterious, valuable reserves on which the other wasn't too proud to draw occasionally... He recognized him immediately, he put him on one side, took him out, lifted him up, examined him...

He held him between his fingers, under his gaze...

He allowed his gaze to fasten on to him, to become attached to him...

It was under this gaze that even if only for a few moments it was given him to live...

Why go on forcing ourselves, trying to go further? We still can't manage to see distinctly, to grasp, to hang on to, to name what we glimpsed when he appeared to us for the first time...

What attracted us, what kept us with him for so long...

We can only assert that it is in him, we're surer of that than ever, we were not mistaken, it's absolutely certain...

But to go on repeating it in that exasperating, obstinate, narrow-minded way...

Without being able to offer any proof, even to ourselves, and that's what matters to us... any obvious proof.

Such as we found with her, when, immediately after that illumination, that sudden revelation, we saw without the slightest shadow of a doubt the first signs appearing in her... the indubitable proof of what her powers give her... a love of herself that is so strong... we had never yet seen one that came closer to perfection.

But with him there was nothing. Nothing you could get a grip on, hang on to...

No look like the one she turned on to herself, a slightly surprised look, overwhelmed, full of wonder. He never looks at himself.

No law court inside him that infallibly administers the laws of Heaven... no precision instrument that enables him without the slightest possible chance of error to distinguish between Good and Evil.

With him, however hard we look, we can see no sign.

It makes you wonder...

No, there's not the slightest doubt, it's there, that's where it all comes from...

204

We're going to get hold of it...

But what with? How?

And if it were actually in the absence of those signs...

Signs that are "conspicuous by their absence"...

That's right... what hope, what support there is in these words that come without being called, that turn up of their own accord, just at the right moment...

These signs are conspicuous by their absence... Their absence is so glaring that it manages to illuminate...

It's still rather faint...

But something is glistening here... in the absence of any look turned in on himself, contemplating himself, full of wonder... He doesn't need to look at himself, to discover anything in himself that makes him deserve to be loved.

He doesn't need to deserve it. It doesn't matter what he's like. No one is capable of judging him.

And he doesn't judge himself. He is sufficient unto himself, and it must be sufficient unto everybody that he is the way he is.

Nor is there a law court inside him which administers the laws of Heaven... Heaven itself cannot dictate its law to him.

He doesn't need to possess a precision instrument that enables him to distinguish Good from Evil.

Is there anything for him that must be called Evil, Good?

In any case, he alone has the power to name it.

The moment he is here, as we have seen, as we know, nothing anywhere has any other existence than the one he gives it.

No one has his certainty. Such absolute certainty. Such unshakable assurance.

Then why hesitate, why go on putting it off, why not make up our minds to name what it is in him, what keeps him so erect, so strong, so tall, what fills him, radiates from him, invades everything...

But "Self-love" is not enough...

Even "A limitless love" doesn't cover...

None of the words that present themselves measures up to it.

206

That shows how far he can get, someone who loves himself with so much genius.

Where shall we ever find a greater genius in the art of self-love?

Above all not be in too much of a hurry, be patient, wait until we meet one on his own...

Manage to lure one away from the others... make sure they can't overhear... get him in a corner, take him by the scruff of the neck and whisper... "You know what it is about your exceptional man, your supernatural man?... He loves himself..." and tighten our grip on him when he starts wriggling... "Yes, he loves himself... and to such a degree... beyond all expression... even 'a limit-less love' can't cover what he feels for himself... It really is genius that he possesses, a rare, a unique genius in the art of loving oneself. Just a minute, though, don't try to get away, that's not all. It's something you must know. It's something you must understand: that's where you get it from..."

His eyes open wide in dismay, in dread, he's a sorry sight... "Don't be so afraid, though... just try and understand... it will be hard, but afterwards you'll see... that love he feels for himself, an infinite love that spills out of him...

"That seeps, trickles, infiltrates into you, fills you...

"That's where you get it from, don't you see, your love for him..." He says nothing...

He completely closes up, he wants to stop the truth entering. But it must... "Listen, you're all infected, contaminated, it's something like viruses that he is propagating...

"It's as if he's sending out invisible rays... they're active even over huge distances..."

This time he shouts... "It's not true, the love I feel for him comes from his obvious qualities. Unique. Incomparable."

These raised voices, this agitation, have attracted their attention. Here's one of them coming up, and then another.

210

How calm they are, how sure of themselves, a little nonchalant... "What is it? What's happening? You seem all excited..." He rushes over to them... "You know, it's unbelievable, it's crazy... It seems that our master, whom we love, whom we admire so much... it's such a privilege, such wonderful luck to be his contemporaries... well, believe it or not, you had no idea, but it seems that what makes him so great is that he loves himself..."

They've never heard anything so incongruous, so insolent... "He loves himself? Thank goodness for that, it would be the last straw if he didn't. Anyway, it's healthy, normal..." "But his love for himself is beyond measure." "Beyond measure? In comparison with what? With whom? It can only be a love made to his measure. He knows his own worth. That's one of the signs of his greatness. It's proof of his lucidity." "But that's not the important thing... it seems that his love for himself spills out from all over him, gets transmitted to us... we love him the way he loves himself, you understand, with a love of the same nature, the same hue..."

They look us up and down, they look haughty, dignified... "Ah, that was what you were saying? That we don't love him on his merits? It's true that it takes certain gifts, certain qualities, to recognize them. Unfortunately it isn't given to everybody... And it must be said that he doesn't go out of his way to be loved... Who

211

has ever seen him make the slightest effort to fascinate, to impose himself? Ah, but what were we thinking of, but look here, but according to you he doesn't need to make a move... He doesn't need to do a thing... our love for him quite simply comes from the fact that he loves himself... through a strange, obscure result of contagion... through an inexplicable contamination... But it's enough to make you weep, to make you die of laughter... How can anyone allow himself to be impressed by such abysses of stupidity, of absurdity?

We step back, we watch from a distance as they give him reassuring pats on the back, hold him up by the arms, he's still a little unsteady on his feet, and they lead him away, turning round and sending us looks full of disapproval, disdain.

We must get him back, he's the one we need, he must be more fragile, more impressionable than the others.

And then, he has the advantage of having been prepared...

But that's just it, he'll be on his guard...

No, he doesn't seem to be, here he is, coming straight up to us as if nothing had happened, just the way we need him...

He doesn't want to look as if he's avoiding us, afraid of us...

We were tactless, blunt. Let's approach him gently...

At the same time delicately reminding him... "It was inexcusable to clash with you that way, to touch on feelings... which in any case are so widely shared... we can so easily understand them... Who hasn't had that experience? Who hasn't been influenced by his prestige, fallen under his spell? People would follow him, people *do* follow him, to the end of the world..." He agrees, he seems calm, satisfied.

Then very cautiously, taking good care not to hurt him... "It rather looks, doesn't it, as if everything becomes transformed under the effect of what emanates from him... what appears then is sometimes unexpected, disconcerting..." He nods... "Ah, that's very true..."

This is where we need to be very circumspect, very prudent...

Extremely skilful... Just one false move...

How shall we go about it?

Lure him over to something precise, concrete, and not too important, on which we can easily pin him down...

The rims of the wells, the little bridges...

The rims? The little bridges? Just like that, point-blank?

Yes, that might give him a slight shock. Jerk him out of his rather drowsy tranquillity...

A salutary jerk... "The what? What are you talking about? What rims? What bridges?"

And we, calmly, quite naturally... "Well, to take just this one example... do you remember how sometimes such things deposited in us for we don't know how long... the parapets of little humpback bridges... what a strange name... the roundness of the rim of a well..." He shakes his shoulders, his neck, the way you do to get rid of something you feel in your back which is bothering you... "Well, all he'd have to do, the man you love so much, the greatest of all, all he'd have to do would be to give them a glance, to raise a hand as if to wave them away, and immediately... try and remember, make an effort... you feel, don't you, as if that old parapet, as if that rim of the well... what has happened to them? what they arouse in you is mistrust, almost a kind of repulsion, it's as if they're covered in a transparent, rather shiny coating... It was his gaze, as if it were a spray gun, that produced that coat of varnish that levels, that flattens... No, just another moment's patience... he's cast a spell over everything that used to belong to you, but it can belong to you again... don't pull back... stretch out your hand, cover it with the palm of the hand you had as a child, whose skin is so new, sensitive...

"Stay behind the others, alone, and when no one can see you, gently run the tender pads of your fingers over the rounded edge... your light fingers brush against it as if no one ever before...

"Or rather, as if it had been filled with everything that has been locked away there and that is waiting for you... the coat of varnish has disappeared, and what rises up to the surface...

"Towards you... For you... It's yours, no one can take it away from you...

"You're home again... What independence, isn't it? What peace..."

It looks as if he's softening, letting go... there's a kind of bliss in his expression...

Of tenderness, in any case...

And then he straightens up, he freezes, he racks his brains... What has happened to him? Where has he gone astray? What has he been compromising himself with? Where has he landed?

He shakes himself and we hold him down by his shoulders... "It's got hold of you again, he's taken you back, he's got you, he's dragging you away from here, he's taking you over there to his place, to the deserts covered with scrub, the disappearing straight lines...

"All right, go there, stay there, in those endless expanses, between the bare surfaces of that cement cube...

"What can it be called, the thing you feel most strongly... it's vertigo... you're sliding towards non-existence, towards nothingness... nothing to hold you back... you want to call for help..."

He pushes us away violently... "That's where I want to live, I aspire to it with the whole of my being... and I'm not being bombastic, as you might think... the whole of my being aspires to be worthy of receiving that strength, that purity..."

We shall have to abandon...

Just one more attempt...

Without any impatience, with the greatest possible calm... "Wait, listen, it's for your own good... that strength, that purity, that's what you see in him when he talks about his life over there... if he had run his hand over the rims of the wells, over the parapets of the little old bridges, you too, with what delight..."

216

Never mind, we have no more to lose, we must run the risk, even if we hurt him... "Come back to yourself, he's hypnotized you, you've been brainwashed... he's got hold of you, he's got hold of the whole world. There's nothing in the world that doesn't carry his trade mark...

"The most famous trade mark. And then you believe that everything he appreciates has an exquisite taste, a quality... that's a very familiar effect, you know, very widespread..."

He flies into a rage. "He's not the one, it's you who are depriving me of my judgment... You're crippling me... You're the one who's dispossessing me of everything... Is there anything in me that hasn't been deposited there by him, that he doesn't control from a distance..."

He turns back to himself... there's terror in his voice... "What's the matter with me? What's going on inside me?... everything's fluctuating, wavering... is it a breath from him that's making everything move?... a breath I can't feel..."

That's where we've got to, those are the results of our need to spread the truth, to liberate, in spite of themselves...

217

To get something recognized although it cannot be recognized...

But which is nevertheless there. That is certain. We can only go on repeating it endlessly...

Only to ourselves. Not to try to make ourselves heard.

Repeat: everything came from his self-love.

Such a love... so perfect, so pure that no one sees it...

In order to see it, they would first have to stop loving him...

Perhaps after his death... Perhaps a long time after...

When that self-love will have died with him...

When he will no longer be there to cover the whole world with it...

To fill everything he does, everything he is, with it...

It will dwindle, gradually...

Or even rapidly, there's no knowing...

It will become deflated, subside...

And then who will take the trouble...

Who will be able to detect it, the thing we can hear... the hissing sound that will be produced as it leaks on all sides... his self-love?

They are gathered together around him... His self-love is flowing from him into them, circulating among them...

It remains just as pure, as intact, as it passes from him to them...

Let's imagine against all possibility that he sees something like an opacity appearing in himself, slight eddies...

Here and there within him something is floating... impurities are in suspense...

Perhaps reminiscences of mistakes he's made, errors of judgment?

But they wouldn't bother him. It may happen that the shapeless, unstable, elusive object he wants to examine will even conceal itself from him.

Would he see, in his past actions, anything that might be called a serious shortcoming? A crime?

These terms, as we well know, are not applicable to his actions.

What has happened to him is one of those things about which people say "it's unthinkable."

But we must try to go so far as to think it... it was in his self-love that there was... for no precise reason, he himself doesn't know it... a barely perceptible movement...

Could it be a slight retraction? a withdrawal?

No, a withdrawal, however slight, a retraction... that's too strong... just a hesitation...

Immediately transmitted to them...

And immediately, there's the same vacillation in the love they feel for him...

222

It lasted only a short time, otherwise, if that perturbation in him had continued, had intensified, what a ground-swell there would have been in them, what a tidal wave...

Couldn't we also see what he feels about himself, which passes from him to them like a cable, a stout rope that comes out of him and encircles them, supports them, keeps them upright, leaning against one another...

If something suddenly began to sag somewhere, to fray, to break, then we should see them collapse, separate...

Any intruder, any boor could insinuate himself among them, give them a push, and they would fall over on all sides...

Stuffed dolls with holes in them through which their love would pour out, crumble into dust...

But we know very well that that won't happen, it can't happen.

That unalterable love will go on spreading...

And how grateful they are to him for it...

Grateful to him for loving himself so much, that's funny, isn't it?

Just a moment, though, it may not be so amusing... Because if he were to love himself less... Because if he didn't love himself...

As is our case...

Then conversely, our lack of self-love... this lack ought to awaken in them...

"It's pathological with me." These words explode, it's as if you'd shouted them... "It's pathological with me," when you leaped outside, when you made an exhibition of yourself in front of them... "It's pathological with me."

We could only look on, cringing, there was no way to stop you...

You're all the time attracted by them, ready to surrender to them, to surrender us...

Ah, here we go again...

225

The same curiosity, the same effort had united us, we'd forgotten it, and now here it all is back again just as strongly as before, our internal tugs of war, reproaches, resentments...

You stood up straight in front of them, sticking out your chest, placing a hand on it... "It's pathological with me..."

Nothing of the sort, you're making it up, we were turning towards ourselves, we said it as if we were talking to ourselves...

Yet it was them you were speaking to, although it's true that it was in a contrite, resigned, saddened tone of voice, maybe with a sigh... "Ah yes, it's pathological with me."

They felt relaxed, comfortable, calm, indifferent, when all of a sudden they saw in front of them, stretching out towards them, calling out... Look at me carefully, look at what I have here, I'm showing it to you, I want you to see it... it's pathological...

You grabbed hold of one of those placards they use and hung it round your neck, you put on the clothes they'd got ready for people like you, you went and took your place in one of their sections, one of their cells, you yourselves shut the door behind you... let them come and observe you through the spy hole...

226

But even before they could make a move, you escaped, running towards them holding out your hands, your palms up, trying to stop them... Wait a moment, don't shut me in... not completely... I've split myself in two... an operation that you advise, I can do it too, I know how to look at myself from outside, I can see myself, know myself... Know thyself, that's right isn't it? you prescribe it... I am capable of it, you see, I come and take my place with you, at the distance where you are, and from there I look at myself with the same impartiality, the same inexorable clearsightedness... I've been able to assimilate your teaching, I've remembered your classifications, I apply your rules, I belong here, with you, I'm one of you... come up, come close... let's look together at what is in me... well yes, it's a pity to have to say it, but it can't be called anything else: it's "pathological."

They begin to fidget, they seem to be torn...

What they vaguely discern, this exhibition, this submission, these sudden leaps, these scissions, these entreaties... make them uncomfortable...

They feel you very close, right beside them, excited, panting...

Must they come even closer, seize you, hold you, straighten you up, try to calm you... "No no, don't say that, it's nothing, it's very common, it isn't anything like what can be called pathological..."

Or must they even, in spite of their reluctance, go so far as to lay themselves bare like you, seize you bodily, stick to you, dissolve into you, becoming one with you... "Me too, you know, it happens to me, it's a state I'm familiar with, you're like me... and there's nothing pathological about it..."

Or else can they give way to their repulsion, get up the courage to stand aside and listen to you in silence...

And put up with the image of the melancholy clown left alone in the middle of the stage, his act didn't go well, he watches the audience hurrying towards the exit, tactfully averting their eyes...

Even you didn't see it coming, you couldn't try to hold us back... You didn't escape, hidden as always when our delegate...

But there wasn't any delegate, who could have chosen him, sent him? We were simply one single element, moved by a single impulse... Seized all of a sudden, invaded, it swept up in us, gushed out of us in rapid, vehement words...

What words?

Impossible to remember them... And even at the time we can't have heard them...

Impossible to recall the people who were listening to them, who were looking at us...

They must have seen our face as they had never seen it before, our features "convulsed with fury," our eyes "flashing with anger"...

And then, when we were calm again... a tornado, a whirlwind dying down... what happened...

It left us so flabbergasted that afterwards, when we were ourselves again, when we were back amongst ourselves, there were no regrets, no reproaches...

Our involuntary "outburst" hadn't provoked what would have been expected in them, not the slightest retort, no hint of a rebuff. And even...

We just didn't understand, we didn't try to understand...

It was one of those strange phenomena about which people say they didn't believe their eyes, nothing we know enables us to explain it...

But now, after all we've seen, couldn't we ask ourselves whether what we made them feel when we stood up in front of them...

As one solid block, closed in on itself.

Nothing that could be attracted by them, sucked in, deformed, transformed, which swells on one side and subsides on the other, all the time shaken by their breath...

Nothing that stretches out towards them to penetrate them, invade them, subdue them, subjugate them...

It swept over them, indifferent to their presence.

We don't know how it came and then we don't know how it went...

A blind force...

A hurricane that made them bow down...

Weren't they a little afraid?

Afraid?

Yes, why not? that's not impossible, it was so abrupt, so violent... they may at first have felt a slight passing fear...

But afterwards, so much firmness, strength, assurance, princely nonchalance, perfect liberty...

reinforced them...

reassured them...

raised them...

They felt a beneficent wave flowing through them...

The feeling it gave them... what can it be called if not admiration, tenderness, gratitude...

For us, yes, us... for a few moments we gave them what is constantly being given them by someone who loves himself...

But not just anyone...

The one who is the most gifted of all for loving himself.

If we listen to it now, that "You don't love yourself" which surprised us so much quite some time ago, we hear it more than anything as a reproach, a reprimand not only for the harm we are doing to ourselves, but for what we are making them suffer.

How good it would be for everyone... how everyone would benefit if we too could feel it, that self-love...

If we could...

We would like nothing better...

We would like nothing better?

Nothing better? Really?